Treasure Ranch

**Center Point
Large Print**

**This Large Print Book carries the
Seal of Approval of N.A.V.H.**

Treasure Ranch

Charles Alden Seltzer

Center Point Publishing
Thorndike, Maine

This Center Point Large Print edition
is published in the year 2005 by arrangement with
Golden West Literary Agency.

The text of this Large Print edition is unabridged. In other
aspects, this book may vary from the original edition. Printed in
Thailand. Set in 16-point Times New Roman type.

ISBN 1-58547-604-8

Library of Congress Cataloging-in-Publication Data

Seltzer, Charles Alden, 1875-1942.
    Treasure ranch / Charles Alden Seltzer.--Center Point large print ed.
      p. cm.
    Originally published: New York : Doubleday, 1940, in series: A Double D western.
    ISBN 1-58547-604-8 (lib. bdg. : alk. paper)
      1. Large type books. I. Title.

PS3537.E4T74 2005
813'.54--dc22

                                                    2005000711

I

His suspicions verified by what he saw, Bob Webster got as far as the corner of the mess house nearest the ranch house before dismay began to creep all over him, to whiten his face and make him uncertain of what he ought to do—of what he could do. Wanting time to think over what was happening before he went to talk with Joan, he leaned against a wall of the mess house, rolled himself a smoke and watched old Miguel put a trunk and some traveling bags into the bed of the light station wagon. The vehicle, with no horses hitched to it, was standing close to the edge of the great veranda, opposite the outside door of the big living room, and to reach the door of his office Webster would have to cross the veranda at that point, where he could be seen from within. He was reluctant to face Joan just now, for she would read the regret and dismay in him. He wondered if she had seen him ride in with twenty of the Parlette horsemen at his back. If not, he was certain she could now hear them yelling and laughing their approval of their visit to the home ranch after having spent a month roaming the two hundred and forty square miles of the Parlette range.

They were certainly raising the devil in the bunkhouse. The horses were kicking up dust in the corral. Not being as observant as he and lacking his knowledge of the impending catastrophe, the men were lighthearted.

He saw Tom Hackett walking along the adobe wall of the big corral, and when Tom reached the huge pilaster of a panel and planted a shoulder there, and spread his legs to disperse the saddle weariness that made him conscious of his sixty-five years; and he saw Tom looking glumly at the station wagon with its pile of bags and the trunk, he remembered that Tom's knowledge of what had happened to Joan more than ten years ago was as complete as his own. He tramped through the heavy dust of the yard, crossed to the corral fence and moved to a point near Hackett, where, bracing his shoulders against the cool adobe, he rolled another cigarette, lit it and puffed slowly. Hackett did not look at him. He was kicking some dust into a hummock, the spurs on his heels softly jingling. His face, seamed and scarred by wind and sun and age, was long and solemn. He spat tobacco juice into the hummock he had erected and said explosively,

"Hell!"

Webster's eyes, filled with the awesome steadiness of an eagle's, flickered once and grew bleak. He was a tall man, with the natural arrogance of physical perfection and the mental urges of authority restrained only by a sense of justice. Foreman of the Parlette ranch at nineteen, after John Parlette's passing, eleven years of his domination of the empire domain and more than one hundred wild riders had increased the importance and prosperity of the landed estate of John Parlette's daughter Joan. But he had sold only his services and his loyalty. The flame that burned in him had always been

6

subdued by the ice of civility. His voice was gentle now, telling Tom Hackett nothing. "Hell for her, I expect," he said.

He tossed the butt of the cigarette away. Yes, Tom Hackett knew. A married man once, having had experience in such things, Hackett had made it possible for Joan's baby to be born with little danger to her—Hackett and the Mexican housekeeper, now dead, and himself, seething with anxiety and pity for Joan, and contempt and hate for Frank Dade. He said, "You'd think she had had enough of him." He looked at his right hand and saw it clenched in the palm of the left. He could feel the clenched hand driving into Frank Dade's face, smashing it. Sounds from the bunkhouse rolled along the adobe wall of the corral and broke around the ears of the two men standing there. Both were watching the open door of the big living room, expecting Joan Parlette to appear.

"Women are not like us," Hackett said, rebuilding the hummock he had kicked away. "Her—she's like her father. She loves the land like he did—and the cattle. Even the hellions who work for her. You've seen her doctor a sick heifer? Hovering over it, petting it—when one heifer less wouldn't be noticed." He looked keenly at Webster. "Or did you ever watch her? A man can't tell about you. You don't hardly seem to notice her."

One of Tom Hackett's deliberate understatements. A sting of his ironical temperament, implemented to force talk upon a subject he could never get enough of. Another attempt to get his foreman to commit himself.

Webster said, "I've given her what she wanted." His voice was dry. A provocative man, Tom Hackett, yet with the wisdom of sixty-five years in his eyes and the cunning of a serpent in his misleading words. Webster added, "She keeps making me think I am not near her any more."

Hackett chewed ruminatively. "That's natural," he said. "After what happened to her she's embarrassed. She's about your age—or near it. You're thirty, and she's twenty-eight. You growed up together. Your paw and maw lived in that 'dobe house down near the Antelope. Near the padre's hacienda. You can see it from here." He watched, but the foreman did not look. "I've seen you and her playing in the creek together—wading and making things out of 'dobe mud. So now that Frank Dade took advantage of her ignorance of life she keeps making you think you're not near her any more." He stared into distance. "Why didn't you or me kill Frank Dade?"

Webster did not know. Yes; he did know. He had wanted to, but by the time he had found out about the baby coming, Frank Dade had departed, evading his obligations. He had slipped away, leaving no word. "Would Joan have wanted him killed?" he asked. His right hand fondled the stock of the gun lying against his thigh. "Likely not," he said.

"John Parlette would have killed him in spite of what she wanted," said Hackett. "He'd have followed and killed him, wherever he went." His lips were tight. "The polecat!" He scratched his head and pulled the

8

brim of his hat down over his eyes. "She having no mother for ten years, in the years she ought to, and her paw dying before she was sixteen. And him not telling her anything about life, or men, between times. And her brothers and sisters pulling out as soon as they could get their share of John Parlette's money—which was plenty. And leaving Joan only the ranch—her wanting the ranch and taking it in the division."

"They don't count," said Webster. "They were parasites, wanting only their dad's money. They took mighty near all of it when they left to go East where they could squander it trying to be something they could never be." He stared at the rolling hills in the haze of distance, seeing a new desolation sitting on their crests. "John Parlette would have killed them, too, if he had known what they intended to do to Joan—leaving her to fight this country alone."

"So she's got tired of the country and is leaving it?" said Hackett. "Giving it all up—at last?" His jaws corded as he looked at Webster for confirmation.

"She got the letter she'd been waiting for," said Webster. He watched the color drain from Hackett's face. Hackett loved her too. But he had known that. "The letter came, after more than ten years."

"You brought it!" shouted Hackett.

"She is not used to hearing you yell," said Webster. "You want to tell her you know about it? She's said nothing to anybody." He stared at the dust of the yard, suddenly hating it.

"It's thirty miles to Maricopa," said Hackett. "In that

distance it might have been burned or lost."

"There was plenty of time to think that over," Webster said. "I'd have been robbing her of the happiness she's been waiting for."

"You know better than that." The tension had gone out of Hackett. They were going to lose Joan. "More misery for her if she goes to him. You know damned well a man like him never treats a woman right."

"She'll have to find that out for herself. It is not my business to tell her."

Hackett's body sagged. "Maybe you're right," he said. "You're a far-seeing man. You brought her the letter the day before yesterday. You figured she'd take a day and a night to think it over. But you figured she'd go. And she's ready. Yesterday you rounded up twenty of the Gila outfit and camped them on the Maricopa trail, knowing that Spotted Elk and his braves are getting restless again. Then she didn't travel and you rode in to find out why. I didn't know what you was up to until I saw Miguel loading the station wagon with her bags and trunk."

Most important in Joan's rigid category of values was the house—or hacienda, as her father always called it. Then came the land—two hundred and forty square miles of it. The Parlette Empire. Then the cowboys— more than one hundred hardy and loyal men of the saddle, addicted to picturesque profanity, reckless conduct, the grass rope, the double cinch, the ox-bow stirrup and elated grins when they succeeded in earning her approval. Then the cattle. Last year there had been nearly ten thousand head in the beef roundup. Then herself. She was not certain where she would finally place her boy Gregg, who strongly resembled John Parlette and who was named after John Parlette's wife, Lucy Gregg, Joan's mother, for the boy was still as much a shock and wonder to her as he had been on the day he was born—when she had begun to realize that Frank Dade hadn't meant all the things he had said—hadn't, perhaps, meant any of them.

All these values had become relatively unimportant to her since the day before yesterday, as through a day and night of thoughtful application to them she had doubtfully weighed them against Frank Dade. Now her trunk and bags in the station wagon, she was ready to go. Yet she lingered, caught in the haunting nostalgia of the past. Once as she roamed through the house and paused for long intervals in each dark, silent room, she thought of days still more primitive than now—the first days, when John Parlette was building the big house, helped by Mexican peons who had fled across the border to independence. She had watched them as they had cut the four-foot slabs of adobe from the perpendicular walls of Antelope Creek, to load them upon stone sleds, haul them to the site of the house and form them into the great fortresslike structure which many times had resisted attacks by the Apaches. John Parlette had felt the spell of the land, beckoning him toward the bountiful rewards to be gained by labor. Vividly she remembered him slogging away building dams, growing windbreaks with thousands of young trees; erecting a system of outbuildings with adobe mud— fortresses every one, forming a great square around the various sections of the corrals. Wisely, before building the house, he had dug a well and had built the house around it so that marauding Indians could not shut off the water supply. So the house contained a well room, with stone for its floor and stone shelves in recesses where stores were kept against the heat and dryness of the outside air. The room was cool and dark, with only one window, and the water in the deep stone-lined shaft was cold and sweet and plentiful.

John Parlette's industry had heaped upon him the harvest denied other and less energetic men who sought riches without effort. The land was isolated in space primitive and menacing, yet its atmosphere was peaceful. Here a symphony of nature's forces produced harmony from dissonant elements. Frank Dade had brought the only discord and she was not sure about him. She was sure of one thing only, that she would let no one know, only Bob Webster and Tom Hackett, who had helped her and sympathized with her and who in more than ten years had not mentioned Frank Dade's name to her. She had endured without growing hard. Without losing her dignity. Without visibly changing. Divulging her thoughts to no one, and by being what her father would have wished her to be.

All the rooms held their memories. Her mother's, prim and neat and comfortable, in which she had passed many days during which she had often wondered why her mother had always seemed so gentle, tired and quiet. She had not the courage to live after Johnny had died under the hoofs of a man-killing stallion he had tried to ride. Another room where her two brothers, Dan and Paul, had grown up, dreamed their dreams, reached maturity and fled to other fields, impatient to be striking out for themselves. Still another room where Gail, who had been pretty, sullen and fiery, had lived her stormy girlhood, only to marry an Eastern man named Harry Lane, who had taken her, temper and all, to tame her. Proud, beautiful, scornful Kathleen, whose room exuded formality, and who had always been nauseated by the odor of stables and corrals, and who always held her fingers to her ears when a calf bawled in the branding pens—Kathleen who, like the others, had been greedily eager to take her share of the division in cash, leaving to her younger sister the ranch and its encompassing loneliness. Perhaps it had been loneliness alone, or a combination of loneliness and Frank Dade and her wistful thinking. She was thankful that Gregg had been born after her father had died and all the others had deserted her.

She passed into the big living room and lingered there, still a bit uncertain. She was ready to go but was held back by a persistent reluctance. Not until she had almost completed a cool and critical inspection of her reflection in a tall old mirror did she realize that Frank Dade's letter was again in her hand. Wrinkled and crumpled as it was it could have been more than a white flash against the smart gray of her traveling suit. Ten years ago it would have been hope and happiness and a song that would have filled the great old house with a vibrant and joyous stirring; it would have created a glowing light that would have sparkled back at her from gleaming candelabra, from ancient glittering panels and from windows that looked upon the somber serenity of the land that had always been home to her. Now the song was muted.

More thoughtfully she studied herself in the mirror. The dark sleek hair beneath the impudent little hat was still soft and young and silky. There were no wrinkles at the corners of her quiet, steady eyes, and her slim, softly rounded body had not yet admitted her twenty-eight years. What she missed was the trusting credulity that Frank Dade had violated.

II

Bob Webster went into the foreman's office, looked around a moment and seated himself at his desk. Some reports he had prepared, some records of which he had been proud, did not interest him now and he shoved them aside. Mentally he was adding some things together—the letter from Frank Dade, with the Tucson postmark; Joan's pensive abstraction after the letter's arrival; the traveling bags and the trunk in the station wagon; the open door leading into the living room through which came occasional snatches of song in Joan's voice which had very little lilt in it; and her step, light and sure, which, because he had heard it many times, he easily recognized.

Suddenly he knew what it would be like at the Parlette ranch with Joan gone, and he turned to stare at the mighty sweep of land disclosed through the open door through which he had entered the office. He lit a cigarette and the glance that slid over his cupped hands was as somber as the land now looked to him. The office was scuffed and scarred; its two chairs were battered and rickety, and the oil painting of John Parlette, from the brush of an itinerant artist, was the only wall adornment except for some dog-eared lithographs and calendars.

Comfortable enough until now. Even John Parlette's austere visage, with the cold, steady eyes that looked at you from any angle of vision, was more grim than usual, as if he disapproved. Every man of the outfit would disapprove if he knew Frank Dade. As far back as Webster could remember, John Parlette's ways of life had ruled his ranch and his people and, so far as such a thing was possible, the lives of the men who rode for him. The riders might raise a little hell, if they did it away from the ranch, but his family was expected to follow his own simple rules.

But if John Parlette had lived he would have seen that his ways did not fit everybody. Children had thoughts of their own. Their own lives to live. They knew what they wanted out of life. How was Webster to guess what Joan was thinking about as she walked about the living room? After the way Frank Dade had treated her she was going to him. What had become of her pride which he had always admired, even though many times he had quarreled with her about it?

He leaned back in the chair and threw his left leg over his right knee, bringing the spurred boot up to where he could see some matted stable refuse clinging to the arch. The boots were crisscrossed with chaparral scratches. The inside of the instep, where it rubbed the ox-bow stirrups he used, was worn almost through, and there were some set wrinkles in the tops where the dust had grimed. This made him think of Frank Dade's boots which had always been glistening and immaculate. And the rest of Dade's apparel. Contempt stirred him. He said "Tinhorn!" and looked around to see Joan standing in the doorway.

She had been there some little time, watching him as he stared at his boots. He was certain she knew he had been thinking of Frank Dade. That pallid little smile; the way she caught her breath; the deeper tint that came into her cheeks, showed he had hurt her. But he sat there, still holding the boot, now rubbing it as if he had been only inspecting it. "Time for a new pair," he said.

"So it is," she said, looking at him in a way she had when she was not able to understand something he said—her head tilted a little to one side like a bird interpreting a call. "And I suppose that's what you always do when you need a new pair? You say 'tinhorn' in a vicious tone of voice—and the boots appear."

He had always admired her courage but never more than now. Ready to go to Frank Dade, knowing he knew she was going and having heard him refer to

Dade as a cheap gambler, she was pretending she didn't understand—and was forgiving him.

Through a window he saw old Miguel bringing up the horses. He hitched them to the station wagon, looped the reins around the whip socket and grinned at Joan. Webster waited for her to tell him she was going. She did not speak. She was not looking at Miguel. She had turned her head and was looking at the plains and the hills stretching to the purple-tinted bases of some crags on the southern horizon. At the granite walls of Antelope Creek where the creek bed became a canyon, beyond which the timbered foothills rose tier on tier to the mountains. At the ranch house and the corrals and the big stables and sheds which in wintertime sheltered the great horse herd. At the blacksmith shop; the harness shop where a saddler was always at work; at the bunk and mess houses and at the cabins in which the married riders lived; at the dam in the Antelope which her father had built, and at the many outbuildings, all constructed of adobe, surrounded, except on the south, by the timber windbreak planted there many years ago—trees that were now tall and vigorous. He thought she was getting a mental picture of it all to carry with her.

"So you are ready to go," he said and saw that the sound of his voice had startled her.

"Yes—almost," she said, not looking at him.

He drew deeply at the cigarette held limply between the fingers of his left hand and looked at the right hand which was clenched. He unclenched it and looked at it.

Would his dream of someday smashing that fist into Frank Dade's face ever come true? Yet he would not try to dissuade her from going to Dade. She had a right to do the things she wanted to do, even to going away to ruin her life. Maybe he had expected too much; maybe their being together so much in their youth had spoiled a romance which otherwise might have developed.

He had never spoken Dade's name to her and he couldn't bring himself to it now, though he knew there were details that had to be discussed. He said, "How long do you expect to be gone?"

She said, "I have no idea."

Of course she hadn't. She couldn't trust Dade; she didn't know how he would receive her. That was what she was thinking, of course. Men like Dade were not reliable. She must know that by now. He said, "If you are going to be gone a long time I ought to know what you want done with the beef cattle next fall. Shall we ship them to Brock and Lee as usual, or do you want to feel out the market?"

"We'll ship to Brock and Lee as usual, of course."

"Under the same banking arrangements?"

"I suppose so." There was a strange lack of interest in her voice. Something that should not be there had replaced interest. Indifference and a dry, almost mocking unconcern which thinly revealed harbored bitterness which was reminiscent to him of one of her bantering moods of her adolescent days, when he had offended her and she was reminding him of his sins. He lit another cigarette and sent a probing glance through the flame of the match in his shielding hands. She gave him a slow, wry half smile in which he could read absolutely nothing.

He had no liking for this inquisition, but remorseless necessity was driving him. He said, "What about Gregg?"

"I haven't told him. He—he doesn't know I have been thinking about going."

"No? He's been with the North Branch outfit for a month." She knew where Gregg was. She was thinking of Gregg now, as she must have been thinking of him after receiving Dade's letter. "The North Branch outfit will ride in this week," he said. "Gregg will be asking questions. I'd hardly know how to answer him. Had you thought of that?"

"That's the trouble," she said. "He has already asked questions. I've tried to keep from lying to him. He'll ask more questions someday—more direct ones. I will not know what to say to him."

"And you thought of taking the questions on to"—he would not speak Dade's name—"his father." He hated to talk about Dade, but for the first time in more than ten years he was forced to it. He saw her eyes widen as if in astonishment over the breaking of his silence. Now he wondered if that silence hadn't actually amounted to cruelty. Maybe if she had had somebody to talk to, confidentially, during the long days and nights of her loneliness she wouldn't now be going to Dade.

Hell, he thought. See how things go? He accused himself, "You damned fool! Trying to do her thinking when you can't do your own!" He took off his hat, crumpled it into folds that made it look like a club and slapped it with a bull-whip report against the boot he had been inspecting. The spur whined and tinkled. But he said gently, "Do you think he will answer your questions?"

"I hope so, Bob."

Her amazing quietness astonished him. He got the impression that when she met Dade there would be no appeal and no humility. Her eyes were still wide, as if she could not comprehend what was behind this lapse from his usual taciturnity. Here was a Bob Webster she remembered, exhibiting some of the violent impulses of his youth. She watched him, stirred by the discovery.

Not a word of condemnation or blame had he ever spoken. He had none for her and he would deliver Frank Dade's personally should there ever come a time when he should meet him face to face.

He said, "Does he know about Gregg? Did he ever know?"

"No," she said. She thought a moment. "Yes," she corrected; "I am sure he did. I think that was what made him go away."

"That was more than ten years ago," said Webster. "If he didn't take you to a real parson then, what makes you think he will take you to a real parson now?"

"I'd know better now. It would have to be in a church, with a real minister." She pressed her lips together and tried to smile. "No more fake justices of the peace," she added.

"That was a rotten deal," he said. "And you would never have known you wasn't married if Tom Hackett and me hadn't found the fake justice when the Apaches were getting through with him. Before he died he said he'd repented and was heading here to tell you how he'd been hired by Dade to trick you. Did you believe that?"

"Yes," she said. "A dying man wouldn't lie."

"That's right," he said. "Dade running away proved it. But now he's near here again. How do you know you don't still love him?"

"I don't know. Sometimes I think I hate him."

He turned his head so that she could not see the savage delight that leaped into his eyes. But he now knew why she had so calmly accepted the epithet "tin-horn" which he had so contemptuously applied to Frank Dade.

He said, "About that question Gregg is going to ask sooner or later. Don't feel bad about it. You're entitled to one lie to straighten the record. You thought you had married Dade. Gregg needn't know that the parson Dade rung in on you was a fake. It wasn't your fault that it wasn't legal. But Gregg will want to know who his father is. You can tell him the truth. You can say that a wandering minister married you. If there was a marriage license the parson went away with it. Tom Hackett and me were the witnesses. All hell wouldn't drag anything else out of Tom Hackett!"

"Or out of you," she whispered.

She took off the impudent little hat. She held it in her

left hand as she extended her right hand to meet his which was reaching out to her as she came forward and stood beside him. He gripped the hand tightly. "You are not going to him—now?" he said.

"I don't think I ever meant to go."

"You always had plenty of sand," he said. "You'd never let anyone know you were hurt." He still held her hand, but now he slowly released it, fighting off an impulse to caress it. He was afraid that in another instant he would put his arms around her. And that might spoil everything. He dropped her hand and took a backward step, and she looked quickly at him, feeling the repressed emotion in him. He had changed. He was not the Bob Webster of their youth. Masterly now. The awkward mannerisms of boyhood and young manhood had yielded to the sureness and confidence of experienced masculinity, and she was suddenly baffled by her comprehension of this development which had been so gradual that she had not noticed it until now. Wonderingly, she watched him. It was like suddenly seeing someone who had been away for many years.

"Tom Hackett will be glad you are not going," he said.

"Did Tom think I would go?"

"He was worried."

"Faithful Tom." Emotion in her eyes was soft and remote, as if she was thinking of the past. It seemed to Webster that she was about to recapture the spirit of those days before Frank Dade had appeared to change her from a lighthearted girl to a thoughtful woman.

"Thank you both," she said and went into the living room. Webster joined Tom Hackett near the adobe wall of the corral.

III

The stage running from Maricopa to Prescott and return was ten miles out of the former town when it overtook the Parlette wagon train which was convoyed by a dozen dust-stained riders. Ten heavy wagons loaded with supplies for the ranch pulled off the narrow road and halted, their drivers climbing down to stand at the heads of the lead horses as they watched the stage go by. The riders of the convoy, strung out over the length of the train, were greeted by the driver of the stage as he passed them one by one. But when the stage reached Number One wagon the driver yelled "Whoa!" to the leaders, cursed the wheel horses who were trying to jump out of their breeching as the brakes squalled and ducked his mouth into a faded yellow neckerchief to escape suffocation from the heavy dun-and-gray dust cloud that instantly swirled around him. The dust began to streak down wind, revealing patches of white sky and an endless expanse of landscape dotted with seas of flowers dominated by tenuous orange ribbons of California poppies, fetlock deep; endless acres of shimmering filmy mesquite and a glittering, gleaming panorama of gorgeous wildflower pageantry of myriad color set in brush, cactus, volcanic rock and sand. The passengers inside the stage, who had been nodding and sleeping through a monotonously dull and drab country stretching over a level near Maricopa, were stifled to wakefulness by the dust and aroused to admiration by the view disclosed to them when the dust settled.

Number One rider wheeled his horse to face the stage. A big horse and a big man, both tall, strong and lean. The horse, prancing, muscles quivering as he balanced himself, poised, ready for a command from voice, rein or spurs. The rider booted, spurred, bepistoled, wearing overalls and a gray woolen shirt, blue neckerchief and a gray Stetson whose brim was pressed well down over his forehead, sat on the horse with easy grace. His gaze searched the stage as the dust settled; and the four passengers, three men and a woman, startled, stared out of the windows of the vehicle to see what had happened. The air was clear of dust again, and was so bright and crystal white that the woman passenger could see the dusky bloom of health beneath the dust on Number One rider's cheeks, the clean lines of his face and the lively interest in his eyes as he now rode forward to gracefully balance himself on the prancing horse as he greeted the stage driver in a voice of friendship:

"Hello, Luke! Still driving stage, eh?"

"Hello, Bob! Yep. Still driving her."

"*Her,* eh? Well, I expect it's all the same."

"What's all the same?"

"Whether you're driving a wife or the stage."

"What *you* driving at?"

"Hardly anything. But I heard you'd gone and got

yourself a wife over in Prescott."

"Yep."

"Too bad." He now looked straight at the woman passenger—who was good to look at—and while his voice was burdened with commiseration his eyes were agleam with keen appraisal. The woman passenger hoped his gaze would linger upon her. Regretfully she saw it pass, to rest upon a heavy-shouldered, bull-necked man with a battered face and an unusually large left ear which was shapelessly puffed and discolored. He was leaning partly out of the stage window, grinning at the rider. His battered lips were genially twisted and his eyes were bright with interest. "Aw," he said, "he's the real goods, ain't he, Mona?"

"Hush!" she whispered; "he'll hear you! He's talking to the driver. Listen!"

"Uh-huh. All right. Sure. But he's the goods, ain't he?"

"Yes, Bat, he's the goods. Hush!"

"Sure he is! I've fought enough men to know a real one when I see him."

"Why is it too bad?" said the driver, Luke.

"Don't you know how it is, Luke?"

"I don't, Bob. How is it?"

"A married man loses caste. He gets to be a back number."

"How's that? I'm onto you, Bob. But I'll bite. How does he?"

The rider was very serious. Yet once again his gaze strayed to the woman passenger who was watching him

25

with a wise smile. "He doesn't know it yet," he said, shaking his head, speaking to himself.

"What is it I don't know?" said Luke.

"That you've been trained."

"Trained to what?"

"To come home nights, Luke. You don't mean—"

"I knew it was something like that," laughed Luke. "Well, I'd stay home days, too, if I could do it and still hold my job."

"You'll tell her I congratulate her?"

"Sure. And that you are envying me too. It's sticking out all over you."

Again the rider's eyes strayed to the woman passenger who gave him an interested smile. The man with the battered face was watching approvingly. Some of the other riders had cantered near and now lounged in their saddles, listening.

"I envy every married man," said the rider.

"Why do you?"

"Shows he's grown up and is ready to take orders."

"That's how much you know about it," laughed the driver. "Why, only the day before yesterday my wife was telling me—"

"It will be that way all through life," said the rider. "You'll make a good listener. All married men—"

"You don't know women," said Luke. "They make you *want* to listen to them." He added, cocking an eye at the other riders, "Indians?"

"Only Spotted Elk raising the ante on his beef rations."

"Why?"

"Too many of his braves getting married."

"That's it," grinned Luke. "Blame it on the married men." He released the brakes. "You're such a son of a gun!" He tightened the reins and clucked to the horses. "How's Joan and her boy?" he yelled. At the rider's nod he added, "Joan hear from her husband yet?"

"He's still spending his time staying away from here," said the rider. The stage pulled out and went swaying down into the ribbon road that wound through the velvet creases of the hills, heading toward the bald prominence of distant mountains which were screened by dust motes thrown up by the constantly moving wind devils that scuttered and gyrated over the face of the land, to build a gauze veil of rose and saffron from horizon to sky. A dust cloud followed the stage, accompanying it to the oblivion of distance. In the dust surrounding the lurching vehicle fluttered a white handkerchief extended from a window by the woman passenger's arm.

Deep in a maze of hills, an hour after leaving the Parlette wagon train, the stage was crawling up a long slope when Luke heard a tapping behind him and turned his head to see the woman passenger signaling him from a forward window. He said, "Hello, ma'am," but waited for the stage to gain the crest of a slope before he pulled the horses down. The instant the brakes jerked the vehicle to a halt a door popped open and Luke saw the woman passenger standing at the forward step looking up at him.

She said, "Do you mind if I ride up here with you? It's stuffy in there and the others are all asleep. I want someone to talk to."

She was on the seat before he could answer. He had known she was pretty. Now he knew she was not reserved or bashful like his wife who would never be bold enough to ask permission to ride beside the driver of a stagecoach. Yet he was not surprised, for back in Maricopa he had been told that she was the owner and star of a troupe of traveling actors; that the show had gone broke, and that she had sent several members of the company East, by train, from Maricopa, and that she and two musicians and the battered-faced man whom she called "Battling" Kelso were taking the stage to Prescott. She was a cute little trick, he decided, with a smooth and easy way of talking and looking and acting—a way of looking at you that made you tingle and thrill with a breathless and stirring ecstasy.

She had hardly arranged her dress and gripped the hand rail as a precaution against lurching when she said, "Who is he?"

"Who?"

"Him. With the wagons. Handsome."

"Oh, him. That was Bob Webster. So you saw him."

"Of course. A girl who couldn't see him would have to be blind all over. Is he married?"

"Him? Gosh, no. He won't look at a girl. Bashful."

She smiled complacently and said pleasantly, "He's important, isn't he?"

"Important? Well—some. He's foreman of the Parlette ranch."

"Is it a big ranch?"

"The biggest ranch, and the biggest privately owned range in Arizona. You're riding on it right now; you've been riding on it for more than an hour, and you'll be riding on it for three or four hours more before you even get to the ranch house."

"It *is* big. Who owns it?"

"Joan Parlette. She's Bob Webster's boss, but everybody knows he runs the ranch to suit himself. He's made Joan worth a cool million."

She said, "Joan Parlette is married and her husband is away." She thought, "Bob Webster is Joan's foreman. A handsome foreman—at least good looking. Interesting." She watched the wild country unfolding beside the ribbon road, and each new vista produced in her mind another decisive factor to the argument which was going on there—whether or not she had grown tired of her nomadic existence, with its uncertainties and its prosaic contacts; and if this country, with its prospect of a change and its possibilities of romance, would not provide her with a more interesting future.

Her decision was reached. She sighed and smiled. She said, "There seems to be only one road through here."

"Only one," said Luke. "This one. It's private through the Parlette range, though John Parlette, Joan's father—and Joan—don't object to folks using it. It's just the other way around. Folks are invited to use it. Every

29

traveler through the Territory knows it or has heard of it. There's never been a more hospitable family than the Parlettes. Folks are welcome there, and they make you *feel* welcome. You come and go and stay as long as you please. No questions are asked. A traveler's money is no good. Folks go there out of curiosity. They stay awhile and the Parlettes are sorry to see them go."

"They must be nice people."

"None better."

She thought of the wagon train. She had been thinking of it ever since the stage had passed it. She said, "Ten wagons! What was in them?"

"Grub, mostly. A freight car full. They make the trip three or four times a year."

"Gracious!" she said.

"Takes some grub," said Luke. "There's more than a hundred cow hands. There's about a dozen Mex gardeners and laborers. They do the stable work and take care of the horses and cattle in the corrals. There's a blacksmith and a helper, and a saddler and harness maker. There's six cooks. There's four chuck wagons and two hoodlum wagons, and the ten supply wagons you saw in the train, and a station wagon and a couple of buckboards. They store about a thousand tons of hay in the fall to feed to the horse herd in the winter if a norther comes on and lasts. And corn and oats. There's stacks of fodder for the breeders and the calves and the yearlings they have to winter. The supply wagons are used in the winter, if there's a deep snow, to haul feed to the cattle out on the range. There's nothing dumber than cattle. They'll huddle and starve, or drift with the wind, before they'd think of pawing away the snow to get at the grass the way horses do. So the boys have to haul feed to them and sometimes drive them to shelter."

"Oh," she said, "*they* sometimes stray from the road too," and looked at him with what he thought was a patient smile.

He grinned. "The road, of course," he said and thought of his wife's ways which kept him steady. Maybe, after all, there had been something in what Webster had implied. You had to be careful or you wouldn't understand what Webster was getting at. This theater girl, here, would fetch him around. "Not much of a road, though it's got a good bottom. Shale, mostly, with some gravel. Once there was a geology fellow out here who said this whole country had once been under water."

"Was this road here then?" she said. "It seems a long time."

You had to be patient with women. "There's a good many things about a road," he said. "You get to thinking of them."

"The road turns off somewhere, doesn't it?" she said. "To go out to the Parlette ranch?"

Light struck him. "So that's what you was thinking about? Yes—it does—after we go through a rock pass in the hills at the head of Bear Flat."

"Are there bears there?"

"Not any more. John Parlette cleaned them out. They pestered the cattle. You thinking of going to the Parlette ranch?"

"I'm going there."

"Now?"

"Yes."

Women could keep a man at home nights, but you could never tell what *they* were going to do. "It's about ten miles," he said. "Ten miles from Bear Flat to the Parlette ranch. It's a long walk. And what would you do about your trunks and bags there on the deck?"

"I thought perhaps you would drive me there," she said.

He shook his head. "Rules won't allow it," he said. "Except in an emergency."

"Isn't this an emergency?"

"More likely it's a man." He had seen the fluttering handkerchief and Webster's straying eye.

She said, "Is there a difference?"

See, he thought. He had known she was tricky. He'd bet that if she got to the Parlette ranch she'd have Bob Webster eating out of her hand. "Maybe not," he said. "Does he know it's an emergency?"

"Did you—when you first met your wife?"

She was right. It hadn't been sudden but had grown upon him gradually. But how about his wife? Had she taken a shine to him the first time she had seen him? Women were sometimes mysterious. This one knew what she wanted. He would have the jump on Webster, for Webster's romance was developing without him knowing anything about it. Funny, in a way. Would she teach Bob to stay home nights? He thought she would. "She certainly had a way of making me see she wanted me," he said. "Was that an emergency?"

"To her, of course. She wanted you. Don't ever make her feel she made a mistake."

"Thanks, ma'am." He began to scan the road ahead, tracing its windings through the hills. "We're about five miles from Bear Flat," he said. "Are you sure you want me to set you down there? It's a kind of lonesome place. Just a stretch of rock and hills, with a spur from this road angling off on a ridge. I ain't seen no Indian signs, but you heard what Webster said about Spotted Elk."

"We shall get off there," she said. "Battling Kelso and I. You can take the musicians on to Prescott, where they can take a train East. I'll give them train fare."

Luke had been curious. "Battling Kelso?" he said. "What's he?"

"A prize fighter. He fought the heavyweight champion some years ago but was beaten. I did something for him and he has stayed grateful. He is faithful and loyal and clean minded. He played Simon Legree in our *Uncle Tom's Cabin* show. Now that the show is broken up, he won't leave me. He has kept certain kinds of men from bothering me, and if there are any Indians around he'll keep them from bothering me too."

"He's a tough-looking man," said Luke. "But he looks kind of simple to me."

His interest sharpened by the appearance of the stage dipping through a shallow arroyo a mile or so distant, the Pilgrim turned over on his stomach, wormed himself down the flat surface of a rock upon which he had been lying half asleep, listening. He drew his rifle after him, clapped his wide-brimmed hat upon his raven-black hair, which had been contemptuously cut where the braid began when Chief Spotted Elk had driven him out, and found a niche in the rock wall, from where, without himself being seen, he could watch the progress of the stage as it moved toward his hiding place. Smarting under the disgrace of his ejection from the tribal communion, still writhing under the memory of the jeers sent after him by the braves, and tortured by the laughter of the woman, his blue eyes, which were the cause of his disgrace, were now glittering with greed.

When the stage had first come into sight far away upon a ridge he had seen the sun shining upon the baggage on the deck. The presence of passengers meant an opportunity to rob. It meant, too, that here he would discard loin cloth and blanket, to substitute therefore the trousers and shirt of the white man, which change in raiment he would be certain to flaunt in the faces of his former friends.

From the belt of the loin cloth he drew a dirty bandana handkerchief with which he covered his mouth to the nostrils, tying the loose ends at the back of his neck over the dangling strands of his hair. Still watching the stage, ready to step forth as it reached the base of the rock behind which he was concealed, he saw the driver pulling the horses down. Astonished, he watched the horses slow to a walk, then come to a halt within a dozen feet of where he waited. Poised, rifle ready, he was about to step out to confront his victims when he heard the voice of the woman on the box with the driver. Through a niche in the rock he could see her face.

"Is this the place, driver?" she said.

"Right here. The road forks over there." He was pointing. "Over there where the pass ends. It's rocky there so you can't see any tracks. But just around the bend there's shale again and gravel. I'll throw your baggage off."

Driver and woman got down. Over the backs of the wheel horses the Pilgrim could see the woman's face as she watched the driver and Battling Kelso drag the baggage off and pile it carefully in the middle of the road. The Pilgrim, sensing that certain of the passengers were going to the Parlette ranch and that presently the stage would go on while the baggage would remain in the road, leaned comfortably back against another rock and patiently listened.

The woman said, "How long will it take the wagon train to reach here?"

"Two hours maybe." Luke was coiling and fastening the straps which had bound the baggage into place on the deck of the stage.

"They will surely be here, though, won't they?"

"Of course, ma'am. Don't you worry. Likely it will be hot waiting, though. Better take a canteen of water."

"I will, thank you. Are you sure there isn't another road for the wagons to take?"

"Dead sure." Luke wiped his eyes with the loose ends

of his neckerchief. He said, "I'm glad to have met you," and turned to mount to the box.

"Wait, driver!" she said. He turned and faced her. With her back to him she bent over and lifted the hem of her skirt. When she again faced him she was opening a huge roll of bills. She gave him several while he stared at her. In his rock concealment the Pilgrim also stared. "The musicians like to drink," she whispered to Luke. "I'm afraid they'd spend this money and have to walk back East. Will you buy their tickets when you get to Prescott? There will be something left for their meals." She smiled at him. "It's been interesting knowing you. Give my regards to your wife."

"Same here," said Luke. "I mean to you—when you get to be a wife. I hope it's Webster. I'll see they stay sober until train time. So long."

He waited for an instant, for she was saying something to the musicians, then waved a hand to her, released the brakes and clucked to the horses. As the stage rolled away, to finally rattle out of sight, Mona walked to the far side of the road, where she shaded her eyes with her hands and looked back to see if she could catch sight of the wagon train. There was a faint dust cloud on the southern horizon.

From the top of the trunk, where he sat idly dangling his legs, Battling Kelso watched her. He said, "Gee, Mona, it's great to be here, ain't it? I was getting tired of that rattler."

"Me too, Bat." She glanced at the rocks behind Kelso and stifled a shriek. Startled by the expression of her eyes, Kelso slid off the trunk and turned to face the Pilgrim, who was just emerging from his rock pile.

He had left the rifle among the rocks and now carried a heavy revolver which looked like a siege gun to Kelso, who was staring into its muzzle.

"White man settum on box!" the Pilgrim told the fighter. "Settum plenty still." He scowled ferociously. "Settum plenty still no hurtum. Get off box, blow damn head off." He pointed the muzzle of the gun at another trunk. He said gruffly, "White squaw settum on box too!"

Frightened, Mona saw no signs of fear in Battling Kelso's eyes. But she could see the powerful muscles of his shoulders and neck beginning to swell and ripple, and as she walked toward the trunk upon which she had been ordered to sit he caught her gaze and blandly grinned at her. "Not so great here now," he said.

"White man shuttum mouth!" ordered the Pilgrim. This was to be more simple than he had anticipated. A fat man, unarmed, and a woman. The money he craved in her right stocking. It had been his intention to kill the driver. Now, the stage gone. The wagon train two hours away . . . He would take the money first. He stepped carefully around the mound of baggage to a point directly in front of Mona and to Kelso's left. Mona was scared but she made a face at him. He said, "White squaw got pants and shirt in box?" His blue eyes blazed and his muscles stiffened as Kelso squirmed.

His *blue* eyes! Strange. It was all strange. The vacant country, the ribbon road winding away into space, the distant hills, the vastness between, the silence which was suddenly crowded with oppressive heaviness. Mona said "No" in answer to the Pilgrim's question and saw Kelso look approvingly at her.

"Want money!" said the Pilgrim. "White squaw got—there!" He pointed to her skirt.

Her eyes were bright with sudden hate. Her face grew whiter than it had been when she had seen him step out from behind the rocks. All the money she had in the world was in her stocking. He knew where it was and was going to take it from her!

"You can't have it!" she shouted. "Bat! Stop the dirty thief!"

The gun in the Pilgrim's hand swung around toward Kelso. But the fighter merely sat there.

The Pilgrim glared at Mona. "Me take!" he said and reached for the hem of her skirt. She evaded his clutching hand and got up from the trunk, to run a little ways out into the road, the Pilgrim following. Twice he grasped at her, just missing her. When she suddenly stopped, almost breathless, he suspected a trick and looked at Kelso, who with patience taught him by his ring experience, nonchalantly waited, with apparent innocence studying the land and the sky. But when the Pilgrim turned again to face Mona she had caught a glance from her friend, together with a sharp jerk of the head, which meant that she was to run toward him. She started to go south, away from Kelso, who was still making a pretense of staring vacantly at the landscape. The Pilgrim leaped after her, caught her within half a dozen feet of the trunk upon which Kelso still sat and grabbed the hem of her skirt. The garment ripped at the waist, came loose, got tangled in her legs as she tried to run, so that she fell face upward, helpless as the Pilgrim jerked the skirt away and tossed it behind him. And there was the huge roll of bills, making a bulge in Mona's stocking above the knee, below a ruched pink elastic garter. Out of a welter of partially nude kicking legs, more pink ruching and lace and pink undergarments, which startled and fascinated white man and red, the Pilgrim could not get possession of the roll of bills. Twice his hands gripped portions of the pink undergarments which ripped and tore as he jerked them; and at last, infuriated, he ran around her as she still kicked at him and struck savagely at her with the butt of the heavy revolver. He missed when she rolled her head aside, seeing the blow coming. His head was bent downward at the instant Kelso's right fist hit him at the base of the brain. It was a hammerlike blow that piled him into a heap, head down against one of the trunks. He did not move as the pugilist stood over him, watching him with curious inattention. Kelso knew what usually happened when he landed on them.

Mona, vindictively elated, apparently uncaring, or negligently disregarding her seminakedness, which was somehow incongruously pathetic and attractive, had got up and was clapping her hands together as she slowly counted to ten. Still the Pilgrim did not move. "You're out!" laughed Mona. She said, staring at the Indian, "If he's dead, and I hope he is, what shall we do with him?"

"He ain't dead," said Kelso, watching. "I figured to hit him hard enough to kill him. He's tough, or I'm losing my punch."

It was a long wait. But presently Kelso said, "He's coming around. See his legs quivering?" He seized the Pilgrim by a foot, dragged him away from the trunk and toward the side of the road, turning him over on his back and looking at him. The Pilgrim now opened his eyes and stared about him dazedly and uncertainly. The bandana had been knocked off his face. "Blue lamps," said the fighter. "Did you notice?" He was careful not to look below Mona's shoulders, for she was almost naked. He was aware of her slight challenging embarrassment.

"Some kind of a breed," she said.

"Uh-huh. He's got a bum moosh. Got a lot of gall. Wants pants. I'd like to work on him for a couple of rounds. He called you a 'squaw.' What's a squaw?"

She laughed, seeing him scowl. He looked below her shoulders. She had a swell shape. She said, "A squaw is an Indian's wife."

"You ain't an Indian's wife," he said. "And never was—was you?"

"Of course not. Goose! I've never been anybody's wife." She laughed again in high glee. She could always tell when Kelso was in a rage, for his lips would come together in a ridiculous smirk. He was smirking now and was very quiet and cold.

The Pilgrim was sitting up. For him the world had ceased spinning, and he was seeing Kelso and Mona

40

and wondering what had happened. Kelso said, looking at Mona, "He lied about you. He's got to take it back."

When Mona said nothing he dragged the Pilgrim to his feet, held him erect with his left hand gripping the back of his neck and stood watching with professional interest until the Pilgrim regained his senses and the use of his muscles. Then he said, "She *squaw?*" and gestured toward Mona.

The Pilgrim looked at him and at Mona. "She squaw," he said.

The Pilgrim's mouth, which offended Kelso, was instantly smashed into a shapeless and awry mass as the fighter's right fist, traveling only a few inches, smeared it. The Pilgrim would have gone down, except that the fighter's left hand, still gripping the back of his neck, held him perpendicular.

"He's stubborn," said Kelso, looking at Mona, who was holding a hand over her lips, though her eyes were vindictively dancing.

"Y-yes-s," she managed to say.

The fighter, still smirking, looked at the Pilgrim. "She *squaw?*" he inquired.

"She squaw," said the Pilgrim thickly and went down from a savage uppercut to the jaw.

After that Mona protested. Then, seeing that protests would not swerve her friend, she turned her back and covered her eyes with her hands, shivering as she heard blows thudding and ripping into the Pilgrim. But after a while she simply had to look. And there was the Pilgrim in his ridiculous loin cloth, swaying and staggering

41

down the ribbon road in the direction from which the Parlette wagons would appear. Kelso was following the Pilgrim very closely, viciously kicking the loin cloth.

Mona dropped weakly to the top of one of the trunks and continued to laugh. She was now crying.

Kelso came back, grinning, and seated himself near her. He said, "I finally got it through his head."

She seemed to be choking and he stared at her in deep concern.

"It's the dust," she said. "It got into my throat."

"Yeah?" said Kelso. "Your eyes too. Dust," he said. "It's mud now. Feel of your cheeks."

IV

The Pilgrim had disappeared and Kelso climbed the rocks out of which the Indian had appeared, to see him riding away on a mustard-colored, ewe-necked pony. He knew Mona would want to be alone and so he searched around and came upon the Pilgrim's rifle which was where the Pilgrim had left it. The smirk again appeared upon the fighter's lips, and he grasped the weapon by the barrel near the muzzle, swung it over his head and smashed the stock against a rock. He heard Mona say "Damn!" and saw her running toward him.

"A man is coming!" she shouted. "Riding a horse. He isn't an Indian, and I'm almost undressed." Kelso mildly wondered why she had called his attention to a thing so obvious. "Open the green trunk and bring me something to wear," she said. She vanished through a

42

passage in the rocks, and over the tops of the smaller ones he saw her head bobbing away. Mentally noting the way she had gone, he climbed out of the rocks and went toward the trunks, trying, from away back in his experience, to remember what sort of undergarments women were in the habit of wearing.

Mona penetrated the wilderness of rocks until she came to an open space about a dozen feet square, floored with basalt black and glossy, so washed and worn by the elements that it had a mirrorlike surface which cast her reflection with astonishing clearness. She passed some time studying herself and was aware of no imperfections other than the huge bulge made by the roll of bills in her stocking. She listened for the hoofbeats that would tell her that the rider she had seen had arrived at the trunks or had passed them. She would hear voices too. She did not hear hoofbeats or voices. When she had fallen while fighting the Pilgrim she had bumped her head on the hard shale of the road, and when she had got up after Kelso had knocked the savage down she had experienced the queer sensation of losing her sense of direction. Now, when she heard footsteps sounding in a narrow passageway that ran in the direction opposite the one she had taken in coming to this place, the queer sensation recurred. Then she heard the clinking of spurs and found herself looking at the Parlette foreman who had suddenly appeared at the opening of the passageway.

She said, "So it was you," and was as calm as she looked. She could not hide all the bare flesh that had been exposed by the Pilgrim's attack so she deftly tucked in a bit of torn shirtwaist which had partially revealed the white skin of her left shoulder and breast.

Webster thought she was almost as pretty as Joan. He ought to leave now with an apology for his intrusion. But he lingered, seeing she had no objection to his somewhat impersonal inspection of her charms. He said, "I did not expect to see you this soon again."

So he remembered her! "I'm surprised," she said.

"Me too," he said and smiled at the bulge in her stocking, above the knee but below the ruched pink garter. "I'm not used to seeing so much beauty all in one day. That makes this scene rare. But ladies with spavins are even more rare."

"You are a flatterer," she said. "And it isn't a spavin. It is all of my accumulated wealth. It's what that damned Indian wanted and the cause of my being reduced to this." She waved a hand in eloquent defenselessness.

He said, "All Indians are damned Indians. And what do you know about spavins?"

"I lived on a farm before I became a show girl," she said.

A show girl. That explained the quiet challenge and worldly knowledge in her eyes, as it explained her indifference to her scant attire. He said, "That's why the stage carried so many trunks."

"So you noticed them? I was wondering. And did you notice the Indian? The last time I saw him he was riding down the road toward you."

"I saw what was left of him. He's a half-breed known as the Pilgrim. I did not recognize him until he told me. He said a giant beat him up. Was it someone who was in the stage with you?"

"Yes," she said. "My friend Battling Kelso, a former prize fighter. Did the Indian tell you why Bat hit him?"

"He admitted trying to rob you. He did not mention that he had torn your clothing almost off."

"So you didn't know you would find me in this condition?"

"No. I didn't search for you but I'm glad I found you."

"I'm glad that is explained. Of course you didn't see my baggage piled in the road? Or me trying to open one of my trunks and running into these rocks so that I could get a chance to dress without anyone seeing me?" She wasn't accusing him; she was trying to see if she could make him betray embarrassment. So far he had been only curious.

"I saw the baggage. The Pilgrim told me about it. I certainly would have ridden toward the baggage if I had seen you near it. I'm glad I didn't. I should have missed—this."

"You are frank at any rate," she said. "Why *did* you ride around the rocks, to find this place?"

"The Pilgrim was afraid of your prize fighter and asked me to get his rifle which he left here, somewhere."

She nodded. "Bat smashed it. I saw him." She listened and heard the sound of footsteps crunching on rock and shale. She said, "There's Bat coming now with my clothes from the trunk."

Kelso appeared, completely filling the passageway which had been more than ample for her. He had an armful of clothes which he was holding out in front of him as if fearful of crumpling them. "Here they are, Mona," he said and looked uncertainly at Webster. When he had first seen the foreman he had liked him. Now here was his charge, partially undressed, with the foreman watching her. He didn't like it. He gave the clothing to Mona and looked at Webster with tentative pugnacity. He said, "You done the disappearing act, mister. What's coming off?"

"Don't get tough, Bat," said Mona. "Nothing is coming off, except some of my duds. This is Bob Webster. He is one of the riders who was with that wagon train we saw. The one you said was the real goods. He *is* the real goods, Bat. Besides that, he happens to be foreman of the Parlette ranch which we are going to visit. I hope you two will be friends."

Kelso's pugnacity instantly melted to amiability. He crossed to the foreman and shook hands with him. "Glad to meet you," he said and looked at the gun lying against the foreman's leg, with the butt prominent and instantly accessible. "Mind if I look at it?" He inspected it as Webster drew it and held it in the palm of his hand. "It's a cannon," said Kelso. "It says 'Colt' on it." He drew another gun from his hip pocket where it had been reposing, stock down. "This here's the one the Indian had. He let go of it when I hit him."

46

"An old Wesson," said Webster. "But still able to go plenty." He returned the Wesson to Kelso and shoved the Colt into the holster on his leg. He saw Mona standing there with the garments Kelso had brought her, waiting. He patted Kelso's shoulder approvingly, with just enough insistent pressure to indicate that both of them were now going elsewhere in order to grant the lady the privacy she needed and doubtless desired. They went through the passageway in which they had been standing and found themselves on a ridge behind the rocks, with an open sweep of country stretching away to the south. And there, not more than a mile distant, was the Pilgrim's mustard pony, riderless, with the Pilgrim himself apparently standing under the low-spreading branches of a balsam. The air was so clear that it was not difficult to recognize pony and man.

"There's the Indian," said Kelso. "He didn't go far. Maybe I'd better go over there and bat him a few more."

Webster said, "He's had enough." He was thinking, "She pumped Luke to find out my name." He added, "Seeing he was busted up some, I stopped him and talked to him. When he told me what had happened I roped him to a tree, staked out his pony and rode over here to find out for myself. Nobody's hurt but the Pilgrim so I'll go back and turn him loose." His own horse was standing where he had left it, the reins trailing. He vaulted into the saddle, grinned at Kelso and said, "I'll take the road back, this time," and jogged away to release the Pilgrim.

47

Riding back, he saw no one near the pile of baggage so he rode through the rocky pass to the spur that Luke had pointed out to Mona, and from the high road that angled from the other he looked down into the wide valley known as Bear Flat. Two thousand head of cattle were down there. Near the willow-fringed banks of Antelope Creek was the chuck wagon, and spanning the shallow bed of the stream was a rope corral, enclosing the horse herd. Some of the men were riding, slowly circling the cattle, observing, singling out the sick or injured. Some saddles, and a few of the men, were lying in the grass near the chuck wagon.

He had an appointment here with Tom Hackett. He was late and thought Hackett would be waiting for him. He moved around a little and then saw Hackett's horse standing in a wide cleft between some rocks, and Hackett himself, descending the sloping wall of the pass. Hackett was carrying a rifle and was grinning.

"Been seeing something mighty engaging," he said. "Had it all to myself. Saw you riding down the road and was scared you'd break it up. You was a little slow, as you always are when there's a woman around. But this time you managed to ride around to the other side of the pass where she was dressing." He watched the foreman's face, enjoying the saturnine smile that lurked around his lips, which Hackett knew as a signal of amused cynicism. "The big man is around there somewhere," said Hackett.

Webster said, "Your imagination runs faster than your charity. She's a show girl and is used to having people see her partly naked. The man is her bodyguard. He's a prize fighter named Battling Kelso. She's a sort of divinity to him. He worships her."

"He wouldn't find that hard to do," said Hackett. "She's a come-hither woman, and he's a sort of simple man. He's got sand, though. Sitting there on the trunk, with the Pilgrim holding a gun on him while deviling the girl, he was squirming to get at the redskin. He didn't dare do any moving until the Pilgrim turned his back. Then he moved fast enough."

"You say your rifle wasn't loaded while that was going on?" said Webster. He looked at the weapon which was resting in the crook of Hackett's elbow.

"I was scared of hitting them—this Battling Kelso, or her. There was a muddle, sort of, with all of them moving fast. I ought to have plugged the Pilgrim when he came down out of the rocks. I'd been watching him for about two hours."

"Any more of the varmints around?"

"Not any. The Pilgrim was alone. Say, he certainly *does* look like that blue-eyed drifter who took the Beaver's squaw into the mountains!"

"The Pilgrim looks like an annoyed sidewinder," said Webster. "Kelso took his gun away and broke his rifle. Feeling as he does, the Pilgrim might come back. Or some of Spotted Elk's braves may be hanging around. Maybe you'd better hang around here until the wagons pick Mona and Kelso up. Looks like trouble on the

North Branch. I'm sending some of the Gila outfit up there."

He rode west on the ridge road and about an hour and a half later he was sitting in the saddle talking with Joan, who had come out of the house at his call. She felt and saw the amusement in him. The house dress she was wearing, a pink-flowered affair of gingham or calico—he could not tell the difference—neat, spotless, starched to a prim stiffness, long of skirt, with a collar snug around her neck and a belt of the same material as her dress, made him think of Mona's fluffy garments and her lack of embarrassment, and of how, perhaps, their selection of clothing symbolized the difference in their characters. If he were to see Joan as he had seen Mona he thought he would wish to cover her up, so greatly did he respect her.

She said, "The supply wagons are coming through all right or you wouldn't look like a songbird in an agony of delight."

He straightened his face, lit a cigarette, swung crossways in the saddle and enjoyed her perplexity. He said, "The wagons will be in about sundown. I'm agonized because the Parlette range is getting flouncy and fluffy."

Studying him, vainly trying to grasp the significance of his words, she said, "What *can* you mean?"

"A show girl," he said, relenting. "Coming along with the wagons. They picked her up at the head of Bear Flat with her baggage and a prize fighter. They had got off the stage to Prescott. Luke Devon was the stage driver.

It's likely he was bragging to them about the Parlette hospitality."

Still puzzled, she said, "You don't mean to say she is fussy and old fashioned?"

"She's just the other way around," he said and Joan was mildly disappointed. He went on, "Oh no. She knows what she wants. She's just extra feminine, and knows it."

"A show girl," said Joan. "I think I understand what you mean. You mean she appreciates her own attractions. Then she must have them. Is she really pretty?"

"When the boys clamp eyes on her they'll all swarm to the home range," he said.

She laughed. "And you?" she said. "Do you think she is pretty?" She watched him.

"She certainly is."

"And interesting, too, I suppose?"

"She has points," he said. He was thinking of the bulge in Mona's stocking, and of his reference to it as a "spavin." And he was remembering her indifference to his glances at her. "Points that a man can't help noticing," he said.

She was wondering why his prompt approval of the coming guest should disturb her. She stored the thought for further consideration.

"And a prize fighter?" she said.

"Named Battling Kelso. Heavyweight. With a bad ear which looks like a mushroom that somebody has stepped on. Thick neck. Nose twisted more than a little. He's all man, though. I think he acts as her bodyguard."

"Why should she need one?"

"I suppose a show girl meets certain kinds of men," he said and saw that her curiosity had been aroused. "She'd have preferences, wouldn't she?"

"I suppose so. We all have."

He took off his hat and ran the fingers of his right hand through his hair. His hair was thick and dark. Years ago, before she had quit noticing him very much, it had been brown, with certain lights turning it bronze. "She'd draw men—where she was," he said. "Anywhere, I expect. Maybe she'd do her own choosing. Maybe some men would think *they* should be chosen. That's where Battling Kelso would come in. I suppose he'd work on them like he worked on the Pilgrim." He put on the hat again and pulled it well down over his forehead. He added, as if he had almost forgotten, "They sent the delayed shipment of canned tomatoes."

"The Pilgrim?" she insisted. "What about him? Sometimes you are positively maddening, Bob." She was remembering how in other days he had sometimes been deliberately evasive when she questioned him. In those days he had enjoyed her annoyance, the way her eyes caught fire. It was the only way he could penetrate her steady calmness.

"Oh, the Pilgrim!" he said. "I forgot him."

"You haven't changed so very much after all," she said, calm again. "I remember one day I pulled your hair for refusing to tell me something I wanted to know. Do you want me to pull it now?"

"It isn't as resisting as it was," he said, reminding her

52

that years had elapsed since the hair pulling. "And it's fading. The dust and sun, I expect."

"It's darker," she said. "And longer than it should be. I suppose it will be down on your shoulders before you get around to telling me about the Pilgrim?"

"Yes—the Pilgrim. He had notions about robbing the stage. Maybe about other things. Pants, especially—in Mona's trunks. Mona had a roll of bills in her stocking. The Pilgrim wanted it and almost tore her clothes off trying to get it. And Battling Kelso almost tore the Pilgrim's face off to even things up. Nobody hurt but the Pilgrim. Mona had plenty other clothes in her trunks." He swung back, astride his horse. "I'll see if the boys have got the storehouse hoed out yet," he said and kicked his horse in the ribs. He heard her saying, "She's a blonde, I suppose?" and looked back at her over his shoulder wonderingly. "Yes," he said; "but how did you know?"

V

A little awed by the immensity of the distance that surrounded her on all sides, Mona, seated beside the driver of Number One wagon, viewed with increasing wonder and silence the gray-white shapes of the Parlette ranch buildings. They and the adobe walls of the corrals filled the mile-wide bottom of a shallow valley whose farther reaches extended to the foothills of a mountain range. She now knew what the stage driver had meant when he had used such terms as "biggest" and "important" in speaking of the ranch and its foreman, and her assurance had almost become diffidence by the time Number One wagon pulled up in front of the veranda of the ranch house and waited there, the driver telling her he reckoned she would be getting off here. She saw lanterns bobbing here and there directly ahead, revealing the bronzed faces and booted legs of men who evidently waited for the wagons to come to unload them; while the dusk floating in was taking on a darker tone as swiftly as storm clouds obscure the sun; and in the ranch house were lights that flickered through windows; and on the veranda was a slender girl in a gingham house dress. The girl was holding a lantern as she peered at Number One wagon.

Mona got down to Kelso's arms and the dust. "So long," the driver called to her. The string of wagons lurched and groaned and clacked as they passed her to go down where the lanterns were bobbing; and the dust, heavy now, erupted around her, forcing her to move toward the veranda where the light from Joan's lantern gleamed upon her, showing Joan her face, doubtful and apprehensive, and her hair, blonde even in the dim light. She seemed to be very slight and small standing there beside the huge and muscular Kelso. Some Mexicans unloaded the baggage and piled it on the edge of the veranda.

"You are Mona," said Joan. "Won't you come up, out of the dust?"

Mona and Kelso ascended the veranda and stood before Joan. Now Mona seemed taller and Kelso more huge. "I am Joan Parlette," said their hostess. "I am glad you decided to come here. You are very welcome."

"Thanks, ma'am," said the fighter. "I am Kelso." He shook hands with her. "I'm glad to meet you."

"I am Mona Wilsden of Boston," said the show girl and sank gratefully into a chair provided for her. Mona said, sighing, "A welcome was more than I dared hope for. We had heard of the Parlette hospitality, and I think that decided us. You see, we thought we were interlopers, for no one in the East would ever think of coming, unannounced and uninvited, for a visit—any sort of a visit." She was thinking, "Joan Parlette! Why not her husband's name, whatever it is?"

"This isn't the East, of course," Joan said. "You will notice other customs which, perhaps, will seem more strange to you. The doors of our homes are always open. I am sorry you had that trouble at Bear Flat."

"You mean with the Indian. The Pilgrim, the wagon driver said his name was. Imagine an Indian with *blue* eyes!" She laughed mockingly while Joan looked at her with calm thoughtfulness. Mona's enthusiasm for her subject waned. She said, "I suppose Bob Webster told you about our adventure?"

"Bob Webster," repeated Joan. "Yes, of course, my foreman." She looked at the lantern on the floor between herself and her guests. "Yes, he told me about it. But come," she said, rising; "you must be hungry. You see, having heard that you and Mr. Kelso were on the way here, I had the cook delay supper. It will be ready by the time you wash and change your clothes."

She took Mona through the living room and down a hall to a door which she opened. It was the room that had once belonged to her sister Kathleen, but now the atmosphere was not so formal, and Mona was delighted with it. There were a bureau of drawers, a great bed with fluffy pillows and a white counterpane; two easy chairs and a straight one; a white wash bowl and pitcher; muslin curtains and ruched drapes on the windows and a heavy rug on the floor, and at the edge of the bed a heavy, glossy buffalo rug.

"Don't hurry," said Joan. "You'll want to rest after that long ride. I'll have someone bring your baggage in. Which is yours, please?"

"All of it except the two brown bags," said Mona. "Please tell them to be careful in handling the green trunk. You see, after the Pilgrim tore my clothes off, leaving me almost naked, I ran behind some rocks and called to Bat to bring some other duds, out of the green trunk. Bat broke the lock and now there is only one strap, which isn't very strong, to hold the lid on."

Joan said quietly, "That was an embarrassing adventure."

"Funny, if you ask me. A scream! The way it happened, I mean. There was Bat, knocking the Pilgrim's block off and kicking him down that dinky little road, mad at him because he'd called me a squaw and trying to make him apologize for it. And there was little me, laughing at both of them and standing there by the green trunk, almost naked. And your handsome foreman came riding down the road toward me."

"Most odd," Joan said. "If you will excuse me I'll show Mr. Kelso to his room."

"Not as odd as what happened later," said Mona; "when I was back in the rocks waiting for Bat to bring my clothes. Your foreman was, he said, looking for the Pilgrim's rifle which the Pilgrim had left behind him among the rocks. That part was true because Bat smashed the rifle. And handsome comes barging into my temporary boudoir through a passage I hadn't seen, calmly looks me over and says the roll of bills in my stocking looks like a spavin." She dropped into a chair, drew her skirts above her knees and displayed her shapely legs, and clacked her heels together, laughing, watching Joan mischievously. "My spavin!" she said, touching the bulge in the stocking. "Your foreman has a sense of humor, hasn't he?" She added, the thought just occurring to her, "But he is a gentleman, isn't he?"

Joan said, "He always *has* been." She was mentally trying to recreate the scene Mona had described. No doubt such an incident would be interesting to the two participants. Was that why Webster had seemed so amused when he had called her out to the veranda to make his report about the wagons? He would be amused—any man would. Mona was making too much fuss over a trivial thing. She had been thrilled by the encounter. Had Webster been thrilled? She said, "I will show your friend to his room. He must be tired too."

She gave Battling Kelso the room that had once been Paul's, the eldest, and Dan's. She pondered that as she opened the door of the room for Kelso. Paul

57

was now . . . let's see . . . Paul, forty; Kathleen, thirty-six; Dan, thirty-two; Gail, thirty. Eleven years ago when she, Joan, was nearly seventeen they had left. None of them had seen Frank Dade, who had ridden into her life before she was quite seventeen, just after her father had died and a division of the property made. Paul had always been overweight and lazy. Despite her father's objections, he would gamble with the cowboys; and once his father had dragged him out of a gambling house in Tucson.

"Gee, this is swell!" said Kelso, and for the first time Joan noticed his left ear, in the light of the wall lamp in the room. She shivered at the monstrous thickness of it, at its shapelessness.

"I wasn't much good at blocking a right," Kelso said, seeing her glances and her accompanying shiver. "Later I got onto it. But then it was too late—I had the ear."

"Why, your lips have been hurt too!" she said. "And your nose! And your eyes are so puffed. Oh, that's a shame!" His eyes, though, had something of the steadiness of Webster's, and she liked them. They were almost as guileless as Gregg's.

Kelso blushed. Sympathy like Joan's he had never experienced. Mona always laughed at his face—kidded him about it. Embarrassment warmed him; instant worship sent a breathless, stabbing ecstasy through him. He had never complained about his battered features, having accepted them as a mark of his trade, though he knew them to be repulsive in the sight of women. He could not remember any other woman who had been sorry for him. After she left him, telling him to come to supper after he had washed and changed his clothes, he closed the door and said, "Holy gee! She's the goods!"

There was a light in the foreman's office, and Webster sat at his desk looking over the bill of lading and checking it with his own record of the supplies that had been unloaded from the wagons and placed in the store-room. His back was toward the veranda, and the light from the kerosene lamp on his desk threw its yellow light on his bared head bent over the papers, making the bronze in his hair glisten and gleam so that it could be seen by Mona on the veranda, sitting in the darkness there. Joan could see it, too, though she did not look as often as her guest who, she soon discovered, was watching Webster.

Hackett was also in the office. He talked little, knowing Joan and her guests were just outside the door. Cigarette smoke from Webster's lips and pipe smoke from Hackett's swirled through the open doorway in flcccy wisps, to trail off into that dcnsity of darkncss which makes a moonless night oppressive. The conversation of Joan and her guests mingled with the noises that drifted in on a listless breeze. After half an hour Hackett's ears detected heavier sounds.

He said, looking at the foreman, "A horse. Walking. Dead tired. Almost bushed."

Webster listened and shook his head. "In the horse corral." He checked a few items.

"On the Bear Flat road," said Hackett, intent. "He's in

that hard shale. The sound will change when he strikes the dust."

Webster grinned over his papers. He said, "Nothing misses you, does it?" He ran the fingers of his left hand through his hair, tousling it.

"Or you," said Hackett. "But nobody knows when you're hit or missed." He tamped the tobacco in his pipe. "You've had opportunities," he said. "You and Joan was kids together. You ran and rode all over the country. And waded and swam in all the water, shallow and deep. When you got aged up a little you both went to school to Padre O'Meara, and learned things about language and the world. But *you* never learned anything about women." The long speech caused the embers in his pipe to cool. He puffed hard at it, and smoke again issued from his lips. "Now there's her," he said, nodding toward the veranda. Webster knew he referred to Mona. "Coming along to teach you," said Hackett. "Another chance for you to make a fool of yourself."

Affection permitted Hackett to take liberties with his foreman. At rare intervals Hackett's resentment over Joan's experience with Frank Dade took that form. He blamed Webster for not intervening.

"Not this time," said Webster.

"There's depth to her," said Hackett, frowning. "She ain't all frills and furbelows. There's a heap of woman there, willing to scratch and bite for what she wants."

Webster shoved the papers away and looked at Hackett. He said, "Padre O'Meara can't teach a man anything about a woman. No man can do that. Nor a

60

woman anything about herself. But if anyone knew, it would be the padre."

Hackett nodded confirmation. He said "Uh-huh" and listened. "That rider has struck the dust. He's heading for the house." He added reflectively, "Curious. The Mexes call him Meario. But he's Irish. There's times when there's the flavor of brogue. That's odd."

"Not so odd, to hear him tell it," said Webster. "His name is O'Meara, but the oilers got their tongues twisted on the prefix and switched it to the ultimate."

"You mean they rolled the *O* from the front to the rear, though you couldn't tell it from the words you use," said Hackett. "The padre has educated men to their sorrow. And women. You and all the Parlettes. And a lot of the hellions in the outfit who act superior in company and raise hell in private. John Parlette brought the padre here and put him in that old hacienda mission over on the Antelope so that the Parlette children wouldn't have to go East and learn all the devilment they've got used to there. All the Parlette children except Joan went East anyway to catch up on the devilment they'd missed by staying at home."

Webster said, "The padre says you don't acquire sin. It's in you. Hereditary. It comes out when you act natural."

There was a commotion outside—rapid footsteps on the stone floor of the veranda. Chairs scraping. Delighted, gasping exclamations in Joan's voice in which the name "Paul" dominated. Webster and Hackett turned and looked through the open doorway to

61

see a horse and rider at the veranda edge, both faintly outlined by the yellow light beams gleaming through the doors and the windows of the house.

"That's the horse we heard," said Hackett.

The rider, a heavy, florid man, with large and prominently bulging eyes, was climbing out of the saddle to meet Joan, who was running toward him. She threw her arms around him, hugging him tightly, while he, his head over her shoulder, was peering at the indistinct figures of Mona and Kelso, and at Webster and Hackett under the lamplight in the foreman's office.

"It's Brother Paul," said Hackett. "Hell and blazes!"

The visitor said, releasing Joan, almost shoving her away from him, "For God's sake, give me a chair! I'm half dead!"

"I'd be willing to help him the rest of the way," said Hackett.

"It's Paul all right," said Webster. "He's tired—already."

Paul sagged quickly into the chair brought to him by Joan, who hovered over him, taking his hat off, brushing the hair back from his eyes, wiping his forehead, stroking his cheeks.

"What a rotten country!" he said. "No end to it!" He threw his arms wide and glared at Joan, as if she could be held responsible. "Sun and sand!" he complained. "The Santo's water hole dried up!" He sat there hunched, now peering at Mona and Kelso, sending occasional glances at the two men in the foreman's office.

"Left Maricopa about noon," he said. "Borrowed that old crowbait from old Bill Nolan. Lord, the man's dried up. Looks like a shriveled lemon. He'll last forever. You'll have to send that crowbait back to him. Only riding horse he's got."

"Too bad he had that one," said Hackett.

Joan laughed apologetically. She said softly, "I'm sorry, Paul. You came in on the ten o'clock, I suppose. If you had taken an earlier train you would have caught the supply wagons which got here about dusk."

"He's one reason I'm sorry Spotted Elk ain't gone on the warpath," said Hackett.

"How was I to know anything about the damned supply wagons?" said Paul. "Or about anything else that's going on around here? It's eleven years since I pulled my freight." He lowered his voice. "I see that old pelican, Hackett, is still hanging around. And your old playmate, Webster."

Joan felt she ought to apologize to Mona and Kelso for her brother's petulance. He hadn't changed much. He was merely eleven years older, heavier and more dissipated. Yet he was a Parlette, and her brother. You couldn't forget that. She said, "Hush, Paul. You shouldn't talk like that." It was a way she had of some-times reproving Gregg, in trying to shape the boy's character.

"Shouldn't, eh?" said Paul. "Who says so? You? Why, you were always—" He cocked his head at her, trying to think back, to remember how insignificant she had been in the family. He started again. "Who were you in the Parlette scheme of things? You never bossed the family around—did you? But you own the ranch now—don't you? And that makes a difference, I suppose?"

She hoped he wouldn't laugh, to further embarrass her before her guests. But he did laugh, and even in the dim light she saw Mona staring hard at him, saw Kelso uneasily shifting his weight in his chair. A quick glance showed her that in the foreman's office Webster was very still, with white lines around his lips, their corners contemptuously drooping, and that there was reptilian venom in Hackett's eyes as he said, "Buzzard!"

Paul heard—and chuckled. He knew how Hackett felt toward him. And Webster. And he knew Joan would not permit violence. "Yes," she answered, "I think it may make some difference. We won't talk about it now. But you are hungry and tired, Paul. I'll feed you and put you to bed. Come."

"You're dead right." He rode stiffly, saddle gall bothering him, bringing twinges of pain visible in his twitching lips. He said to all of them, "Don't try to ride thirty miles after eleven years of holding down the plush upholstery," and tried to see Mona more clearly.

Mona pretended not to hear and listened to Joan, who was presenting him, "My eldest brother, Paul. Miss Mona Wilsden."

Mona bowed stiffly.

"Please-to-meecha," grunted Kelso, looking past Paul and holding his hands behind him. The right hand was clenched.

64

"Neighbors?" Paul inquired. He could see Mona's face more clearly now.

"Miss Wilsden is an actress," said Joan. "She and her friend are on their way to Prescott. They stopped off here for a visit."

Paul was studying Mona's face and finding it attractive. He said to Joan, "Her friend, eh? What is he, a drummer?"

"Mr. Kelso is a prize fighter," said Joan.

Paul straightened and peered closely at the fighter. "By Jove, that's right! You're Battling Kelso! Why, I've seen you in the ring!" He stepped back a little, respectfully. "So you're the little girl's friend?" he said.

Kelso said, "That's right, mister. And I mean—friend. Understand?"

"Oh, of course," said Paul, looking at Joan. "Nothing personal intended." His voice had a laugh in it. "It's great!" he said. "A show girl and a pug. A perfect setting for Kathie and Gail when they get here next week. They'll be charmed, I assure you. And their Newport and Bar Harbor friends will be green with envy when they hear of it."

Joan gasped, "Next week!"

What her sister would say or think about Mona and Kelso staying at the ranch concerned her very little, but that they were coming at last was news that set her heart to thumping with gladness. She loved them and longed for them. Next week, after all these years, they were coming!

Seeing the happiness in Joan's eyes, Mona smiled.

But Mona was thinking, "My God! I hope they are not like this chump!"

Excitedly Joan said, "Only Kathie and Gail? What about Gail's husband—Harry Lane? And Dan? Aren't they coming too?"

Paul said, "Harry Lane is dead. He died the year after he and Gail were married. Kathie could never find anyone sporty enough for her until she picked up a clubman with more dough than reputation, who divorced her with a settlement that should have lasted her. She ran through it in two years. She's flat broke. So is Gail. And so am I. So we're looking for a grubstake."

Joan smiled through the shock. "That's too bad, Paul. But there is room enough here for all of us."

"That's what we thought. Oh, we looked you up. We wouldn't have thought of coming back unless we knew you had sufficient kale."

"Kale?"

"Iron men," said Kelso. "Dough. Money."

Joan said quietly, "What about Dan? Is he without money too?"

"Dan's dead. He died about three years ago."

Joan was silent, stricken. Mona pitied her. In the foreman's office Hackett said, "Her favorite brother! Damn their mangy hides!"

"You didn't write to me about it," Joan said. "You have never written!"

Paul shrugged his shoulders. Joan turned swiftly to the fighter and said steadily, "Mr. Kelso, Paul will want his own room, I suppose—his room and Dan's. If you

66

don't mind we'll move you to another."

"Sure!" said Kelso. He followed Joan into the house and down the left wing to the room she had previously assigned to him. She showed him another, just opposite, and went in to look it over while he carried his bags in.

"Aw, say," he said as going out she paused and leaned against a doorjamb. "That was a rotten thing, not letting you know about your brother Dan."

"It doesn't matter," she said. "They always—"

"Treated you like a dog," he said. "Anyone could see that. Say the word and I'll go out there and knock his block off!"

She faced him, smiling with quivering lips. "He is my brother, Mr. Kelso."

Kelso smirked, though his eyes were bright with admiration. "You're game as a pebble, Miss Joan," he said. "You can take it without letting them know you are groggy."

He watched her go down the hall, then closed the door and began to walk back and forth in the room, his puffed lips working soundlessly. Suddenly he stopped, said "Jeez!" and swung both fists with terrific force, as if fighting with someone.

VI

"Folks are like that," said Tom Hackett. "Only more so." A horsehair rope, braided, was lying near him on the scorched ground near the campfire, its coils glistening from frequent rubbings with wet rawhide. He stopped shoving a harness maker's needle back and forth through the honda he was shaping at the end of the rope. He went on: "If a thing you see don't interest you right away you don't pay enough attention to it to find out what it is." He pulled a plug of tobacco, a conical stone pipe and a jackknife from a pocket. He cut a slab of tobacco from the plug, rolled it between the palms of his hands, licked the knife blade with his tongue and put tobacco and knife back into the pocket. He said, between puffs at the pipe, looking at Gregg over the match flame, "There's that cooney, now, under the chuck wagon. You've seen it a lot of times on all your maw's wagons but you never asked what its name was. You wasn't interested." He puffed, making grunting noises. Through the smoke that drifted upward into the windless dusk he watched a moonlit ridge where late that afternoon he had seen a silhouetted Indian, rigid and motionless, blanketed, his braid hanging straight down as he stared at the cattle in the valley bottom— and no doubt counted the riders guarding them. Hackett had been so close, behind a thicket of alder and scrub cedar, that he had clearly seen the roach of the brave's hair and the parted hanks that came down to meet the braid. A Maricopa Apache. Again now he spoke to Gregg. He said, "Folks take too much for granted." Once more he thought of the Indian. After watching until the Maricopa disappeared, he had swung around and slipped up a dry wash to a far, brush-screened hilltop, to see Indian lodges with their hide-covered walls and their crossed center poles dotting a sheltered level of the Antelope where the stream doubled before it flowed down to the flat. He was surprised to see them there, for the last time he had heard of them they were on the North Branch. It was not a war party, for they had brought their women and children. Some of the ponies were still rigged to travois poles. He went back to his subject, saying, "Some cook with an idea of saving his legs invented the cooney. The cook who first built a cooney had picked up dry wood as he drove along with his chuck wagon. He put the wood into the cooney where it stayed dry. A cooney is nothing but a dry hide tied under the bed of a wagon. But some cook had noticed things."

He worked again with the honda. At dusk he had doubled the night herd crew, against any chance that the Maricopas might take some steers without permission. One success would make them bolder. If trouble was to come it was just as well to have it arrive before they got too arrogant. But he'd have to get Gregg away from here, back to the ranch house where he would be safe.

"This rope is finished," he said, tossing it into the boy's eager hands and seeing how delighted he was. "There's a lot of life in a horse's tail," he said. "But when they get too dry they turn brittle. Then they are not so strong. If I was you I'd ride for the home ranch tomorrow and spend a great deal of my time polishing the rope with damp rawhide. Maybe I'd keep throwing it at a snubbing post in a corral to limber it up and get the honda to running smooth. It takes quite awhile to limber a rope to where the noose won't kink."

Gregg said, "Thank you, Tom," and smiled at the ropemaker. He added, "Gee! You started it last fall, didn't you? Making a horsehair rope takes a long time. But it's a beauty!"

"You like it, eh?" Tom said. He liked the kid. As well as he liked the kid's mother. "How many horses' tails went into that rope?" he asked and got a shake of the head for an answer. "I don't know either." He liked to see pride of ownership in Gregg's eyes. The kid reminded him of John Parlette. His young manliness was a counterpart of the dead owner's character.

"I'll ride in tomorrow morning," said Gregg.

"I'll ride along with you," Hackett said. "I've got to go in anyway." Thinking the inducement of rope limbering might not be quite enough, after a night's reflection, he added, "There's another reason why you ought to go in. Your maw's got company."

"Who?"

"Nobody you know. Your uncle Paul from the East. And a show girl. And"—he kept the ace in the hole for the last—"a prize fighter."

"Gosh!"

"A heavyweight prize fighter. His name is Battling Kelso. Ever hear of him?"

"Sure. He fought the champion. He got licked but he made a good fight. Gosh!"

Hackett now made it strong. "Maybe you could get him to give you boxing lessons. He's a nice feller."

"Did he bring boxing gloves?"

"He brought two valises with him," said Hackett.

"And he don't wear many clothes. Just some light shoes, a pair of pants and a funny kind of shirt without any sleeves to amount to anything. It's likely he's got boxing gloves. There's another thing. Two of your aunts are coming tomorrow—your aunt Kathleen and your aunt Gail. Webster and some of the boys are going to Maricopa tonight to meet tomorrow morning's train. They're taking the station wagon to bring them to the ranch."

Gregg carried the new rope to a spruce near the bank of the creek where his saddle was hanging from a low limb. He lashed the free end of the rope to the saddle horn, threw its coils over, got his blanket from the bedroll and went back to the fire where Hackett was knocking the ashes from his pipe.

Midafternoon came before they got started toward the ranch house. Hackett had circled the herd and had given orders to slowly edge it down to where the valley broadened and flattened, later to meet the level country beyond. To various lounging riders he spoke of the presence of the Maricopas, and at last rode back to the chuck wagon where, with Gregg watching from a distance while saddling his pony, he told the cook to hitch up and begin to drift downstream with the herd. The cook was warned to move leisurely. Gregg had watched the wranglers hazing the horse herd down the creek, and as he and Hackett racked through the valley toward a sandy arroyo that looked like the bed of an ancient watercourse, he several times glanced inquiringly at his friend. Later in the afternoon, following a shallow ravine that led to some timber above, he spoke. "Won't they think we are afraid of them, Tom?"

Hackett's start was inward but he stopped chewing his tobacco. He said, "Who will think we are afraid?" and looked at Gregg.

"The Maricopas," said the boy.

"What Maricopas?"

"The ones that are camped above the head of the flat. Yesterday afternoon I saw you ride up that dry wash to look at them. While you were telling off the men for night herd duty I rode up the wash and had a look at them too. There's not so many of them. I counted twenty-two braves. Spotted Elk is there too. And I saw that brave on the ridge watching the herd."

Hackett grinned. The way the kid had acted no one would have known he knew anything about the presence of the Maricopas. He said, "I thought I was being slick last night when I was shooting off about the cooney. You do notice things."

The ravine angled away from the flat. It ran through a cedar brake as it gradually ascended to higher country, and the brush along its edges grew thicker and taller. It doubled sinuously, widening always until it merged with a wooded slope that led to the road over which the Parlette wagon train had traveled on the day it had brought Mona and Kelso to the ranch.

"The Maricopas were near the North Branch when I left there Tuesday with Jardine," said Gregg. "Webster sent some of the men of the Gila outfit up there. Was

72

he expecting trouble?"

Hackett looked at the sun. He was reluctant to continue this subject. "Webster and the station wagon ought to be along pretty soon now," he said. "No—no trouble. He aims to avoid it. At the same time he won't take any orders from Spotted Elk."

"Orders?"

"I expect you've heard about it—or you've guessed it. Spotted Elk has been kicking about the beef ante. The agreement your maw made with him last year was a steer a week. Now he wants two. Claims the hunting is bad. Fact is his braves are too lazy to hunt. Spotted Elk wants your maw to come to him for a powwow. Webster won't let her do it. It's Spotted Elk's place to go to see her. Think of her running to make a deal with a damned Indian!" He looked hard at Gregg, his eyes narrowing, and suddenly pulled his horse down, motioned Gregg to do likewise, threw his head up and sniffed the slight breeze that wandered up the ravine. An eagle feather showing above a manzanita clump at the road's edge above caught his attention before he had time to look down the ravine. He whispered "Scoot!" to Gregg as he wheeled his horse to go back the way they had come, but with the movement he saw two Maricopas coming up, riding bareback as they always did. A roan and a paint horse wearing rawhide hackamores. Funny how a man would notice such things at a time like this. He backed his horse into the trees at the edge of the ravine, whipped his big gun from its holster on his leg, feeling Gregg near him, seeing a sunflash from the polished blue of the gun in the boy's hand. Gregg was always rubbing and oiling the weapon, and at times, while riding, drawing and pointing it. Now he suspected Gregg knew what was up.

The timber along the edge of the ravine was too thick for running. It would have to be fought out right here. But he wanted Gregg to get out of it clean, so he yelled for him to stay where he was and jumped his own horse down the ravine, straight at the two Maricopas who were coming up. His Colt poised for a shot, he saw the right hands of the two Indians raised in the peace sign, so he reined in, warily watching them. He heard Gregg calling to him, saying, "They're friendly, Tom!" and glanced swiftly up the slope to see two other Maricopas standing near the manzanita clump, just where the slope merged with the road. They, too, were making the peace sign. He saw how it was and was mad clear through. Knowing he was in charge of the outfit, they had watched him, wanting to talk about their beef rations. Likely the brave he had seen on the ridge yesterday afternoon had seen Gregg, who was known to them.

The two who had ridden up the ravine had stopped at a little distance, far enough away to keep their ponies from wrangling with his, but near enough for him to smell them and to see the thong-wrapped handles of tomahawks stuck in the girdles of their breech clouts, the heads at their backs. They bore rifles, a long Sharps and a Wesson, under their left arms, the muzzles pointing downward. The two who stood near the manzanita clump had no rifles. All their faces were inscrutable except Gregg's, who watched Hackett to interpret his movements and to catch any signs he might give.

The Indian on the paint horse wore two feathers in his hair and a frontlet band of elk teeth on his forehead where the hair began. Dirty buckskin leggings ran upward to his knees, and his beaded moccasins were scuffed almost through at the toes.

"How!" he said.

"How!" said Hackett. Gregg was silent, watching.

"Me Two Feathers. Me want talk with white brother," said the rider of the paint horse in understandable English.

"Sure," Hackett agreed. But he wouldn't talk here where they had him and Gregg between two fires. He jerked a thumb toward the road above. "Up there on the level," he said. He motioned the Maricopas forward. They rode past him while he stayed Gregg, and as Gregg ascended he sent his own horse up with a rush that quickly took him to the boy's side. "Let her go!" he said to Two Feathers.

The Indians were solemn. Two Feathers held up two fingers of his right hand, separated, and said, "Maricopas want two beef. One no good."

After all, this was just palaver—a dicker for additional food. A bluff perhaps. They might be fearful that the one steer a week would be denied them. They did not intend to force things. Or did they? He watched Two Feathers' eyes. Their beady depths could not be

75

read. He would find out what their temper was—their intention.

He said, grinning, "Why don't Maricopas hunt for game?"

"Hunt no good," said Two Feathers. "Want two beef!" An angry flash crossed his eyes. So their hearts were not entirely peaceful! Their demands refused, they would turn warlike. Hackett tickled the belly of his horse with the touch of a rowel, making him jump. Gregg's pony backed away and Hackett edged in front of him.

Hackett had no authority to settle it. He said, "You'll have to talk to Joan Parlette," and sought to swing his horse to one side, to pass them. He had a slight hope that the gesture would end the parley. Two Feathers' companion jumped his roan over, and the two others, afoot, stepped in front of Hackett's horse, and Hackett saw it would not be so simple as he had thought.

"She no come to talk with Maricopas?" said Two Feathers.

"Sure not. You go talk to her. Have Spotted Elk go—he's your chief."

Two Feathers shook his head decisively from side to side. "Spotted Elk no go to squaw. Squaw come to Spotted Elk. Spotted Elk big chief. Want two beef. Want white squaw come!"

"No!" said Hackett, shaking his head. The Maricopa on the roan horse kept trying to edge around to his right. He stopped that by seeming to accidentally keep his own horse in the way. Both animals, their ears laid back, their teeth bared, made the maneuver difficult;

76

and when Hackett saw it was their intention to surround himself and Gregg, and that already he had to turn his horse sideways to Two Feathers and the dismounted Indians, he began to understand they were trying to separate him from the boy.

"White squaw no come, we take white boy," said Two Feathers and drove his paint horse toward Gregg's pony. Now the roan squealed in fury as its rider forced it against Hackett's horse; and in the resulting melee the dismounted Indians were lunging forward, snatching at Gregg's bridle reins. The rider of the roan horse was trying to swing the muzzle of his rifle up to bear on Hackett, and Hackett, who had shoved his Colt down his leg when he thought the Maricopas might prove to be friendly, now jerked the weapon loose. Its explosion made the roan rear backward in fright, and as the big gun kicked upward the Maricopa jerked sideways and tumbled into the heavy dust of the road. The roan galloped off, bucking and squealing, and Hackett, aiming from the hip at Two Feathers, saw the Indian, close, reaching for Gregg. The boy, who had been waiting for his friend to take the initiative, had drawn his gun with Hackett's movement. As Two Feathers reached for him, swinging near, he smashed the long barrel of the forty-ounce weapon down upon the Indian's forehead near the elk's tooth band. As Two Feathers reeled, to pitch off the paint horse after the animal had taken not more than two or three jumps, Hackett saw a crimson streak appear on the red man's forehead. The dismounted Indians began to run toward the timber in which they had left their horses. Hackett spurred after them, Gregg riding close behind, not so bloodthirsty as Hackett, who was raging. The foremost Maricopa reached the timber, disappeared into it. The second spun around and dived crazily into the road as Hackett's vengeful bullet struck him, and as man and boy pulled up, to hear the escaping brave's pony crashing through the natural forest barriers, they saw blood welling up from the bronzed back of the Indian lying face down in the road.

Awed, Gregg exclaimed, "Gee, Tom, in the heart!"

Hackett said, "An Indian ain't got any heart," and wheeled his horse to go back where Two Feathers was lying, face up, close to a clump of greasewood. Gregg rode close behind Hackett. "You sure busted him, kid!" said Hackett. "Saved me killing him. He'll wake up with a headache, and then he'll go back to camp and tell Spotted Elk that you and me don't think much of this hostage business." He looked at the paint horse standing near, and at a bay pony running hard over a distant level, his rider showing only a leg and an arm over the animal's back. "We'll have to get out of here," he said. "They'll be buzzing around pretty quick." He turned to take a final glance at Gregg's victim lying near the greasewood clump, with his elk's tooth frontlet band and his foolish feathers. Man and boy now heard the clip-clop of hoofs near by. They watched a dust cloud traveling toward them from east to west along the road to the ranch, and then they saw the Parlette station wagon, convoyed by several Parlette riders, coming toward them.

VII

Kathleen would not step down into the dust of the road to look at Two Feathers lying near the greasewood. But Gail got out and stood close to him as he got up, dazed bewilderment in his eyes, to stare at her and at the driver of the wagon, who vindictively watched him, and at the several cowboys who were clustered around Webster and Hackett a little distance away.

"What a beastly face!" said Gail. "He's had smallpox."

"Don't look at him then," Kathleen said, shuddering. She turned her back.

Ranch born, Indians were no novelties to the returning sisters of Joan Parlette, for they could remember days when Apaches were more numerous than now, and soldiers fewer. With the detachment of casual interest they had read of cavalry posts in Arizona being augmented or newly created, and of Apaches being herded to reservations. Yet dead Indians had been vastly more appreciated by John Parlette than live ones, and this pleasant philosophy had descended to his daughters. Without a pulse of pity they watched Two Feathers rise and stagger to his paint horse, to climb upon its back and ride away, neglecting to search for his rifle which, when he had tumbled from his horse, had hurtled from his hand into some juniper bushes. The sisters were more interested in Bob Webster, who was now questioning Tom Hackett.

"Twenty-two braves, you say?" said Webster. "That's about all there were at their North Branch village. They've been drifting away from Spotted Elk. Some are roaming Tonto Basin, and some are up the Hassayampa, just this side of old Fort Whipple. The braves that are left are too lazy to hunt or fight. I don't think we will have any more trouble with them. Yet just to be sure they don't get the jump on us you men can join the Bear Flat outfit, temporarily. You can go back with them, Tom. Tomorrow you can send a man to the North Branch to bring back the Gila men who went up there last week. Don't go out of your way to look for trouble, but if trouble comes, let them know about the brand you keep on hand. Got plenty of ammunition?"

"Plenty. In the chuck wagon. So long." He rode down into the ravine with the men of the wagon convoy. He turned in the saddle and shook hands with himself, with Gregg watching him. He called back to Gregg, "You're the seeingest kid, and the bustingest. Just like John Parlette, and your maw. If you put on the gloves with Battling Kelso sock him in the kisser for me. And you—you old hawknocker"—he was now grinning at Webster—"you ain't the kissable kind. But you might be. What you need is a burr under your saddle!"

"He made me a horsehair rope," said Gregg, proudly showing it. "He's so quiet and kind and deep. He keeps you guessing about what he's thinking. Why did he say you need a burr under your saddle?"

"Thinks I need bucking up," said the foreman. "And maybe I do. Yes—he keeps you guessing."

They rode back to where Kathleen and Gail were waiting in the station wagon. The sisters had seen the two Indians lying in the road, and had tried to hear what Webster and the other men had been saying. Only Hackett's voice, from the ravine, had reached them, very faintly.

"Wasn't that Tom Hackett?" said Kathleen.

Webster said "Yes" and motioned the driver to proceed. There would be no other wagons coming along the road, and the Maricopas would return for their dead. He rode beside the wagon now, with Gregg beside him.

"Why didn't Hackett speak to us?" said Kathleen.

"Tom's bashful," said Webster. "Besides, he wasn't around much when you were at home."

"That's absurd! He was married at the Parlette ranch. They had two children, but both of them died. Then his wife." She knew Hackett had never liked her and she had always been annoyed by his speculative glances at her. She had always suspected Hackett knew her better than she knew herself, and the thought had irked her.

Until now Webster had ridden far ahead of the wagon. He hadn't wanted to answer questions—wouldn't answer them. Now, because he felt more responsible than ever, he had to ride near the wagon. And the questions came. He fended off some, the important ones which would have provided the girls with information about Joan and the ranch. He answered others. Yes, Padre O'Meara was still at his hacienda on the Antelope. The Apaches were always troublesome. He had been the Parlette foreman for about eleven years. Yes,

Joan had appointed him. Was it true that Joan had grown wealthy? A Chicago livestock man, visiting Newport, had told her so, said Kathleen. He said, "Was he a dealer in bulls and bears?" and succeeded in keeping his face straight.

"You *are* naïve, aren't you?" said Kathleen, but there was doubt in the probing glance she gave him. He hadn't answered her question. He was good looking enough to arouse her interest, and she saw Gail critically watching him as he rode along, tall and loose in the saddle and very graceful. He had a striking profile, and the raw bronze of his skin gave him a wild look— like an Indian. She thought things would be rather dull here and that it would be fun to tame him. Remembering him as a reckless daredevil in the old days, when her father recounted his exploits as a bronc buster, a fearless fighter of Indians, a top roper, a tireless rider who had been respected far and wide for his wizardry with a six-shooter and a rifle and his cold nerve in a crisis, she saw that age had taken the edge off his ebullience to fashion him into an easygoing, quietly confident and dependable foreman who was liked and respected by his wild riders and who was responsible for Joan's success with the ranch. She had quietly questioned the driver of the station wagon, to find him taciturn but very respectful when she mentioned Joan.

It wasn't until Gail exclaimed, "Oh, look at that beautiful kid!" that she noticed Gregg. Then she said, "He *is* beautiful, isn't he? All cowboys are alike until you look closely at them. He's dressed just like the others were.

And he carried a six-shooter and a rifle. Imagine that! And he's just a boy, isn't he? He can't be more than twelve—thirteen or fourteen at most." They watched him as he jogged along, an easy, graceful rider, talking with the foreman who had spurred ahead to escape further questioning.

Gail said, watching Gregg, "He reminds me of someone. Dan!—when Dan was his age. Why, he looks like Dan, doesn't he? And like Father! Isn't that remarkable?"

"Very," said Kathleen. "Yes. But of course he doesn't. We've simply forgotten."

Gail said, "I'm going to find out who he looks like," and called to the driver who looked back at her. "Stop!" she ordered. "We want to rest."

The horses were pulled down, and the driver slid out of the seat, stretched himself and leaned against the right fore wheel. Gail got out first, and, seeing no dust on the shale surface of the road, Kathleen followed. Webster and Gregg rode back to see what was wrong, and Webster suspected the truth when he saw the sisters staring at Gregg.

"My, what a young cowboy!" said Gail. She thought he had the Parlette eyes, with their clarity and serenity and their quiet, meditative calmness. Webster had turned his head but was listening.

"You can't be over twelve or thirteen," said Kathleen. "Are you?"

"I'm going on eleven, ma'am," answered Gregg. "Are you Aunt Kathleen or Aunt Gail?"

Gail gasped and Kathleen said, "Well, of all things! Who are you?"

"I'm Gregg Parlette, ma'am," he said and was curious when they showed astonishment.

They looked significantly at each other while Webster hid a satirical smile with a hand. It was awkward for the boy, so he said dryly, "He is Joan's boy," and let them see his smile.

Kathleen was trying to read his expression. She said, the acid of doubt dripping from her voice, "We hadn't heard about Joan being married!"

Webster said, "That's strange. She sent that report out, along with the one about her wealth," and kicked his horse in the ribs, Gregg following him, while the driver herded the passengers aboard and spoke to the horses.

"I think he was trying to be sarcastic," Kathleen said, staring after the riders. "And—if Joan *is* married, why does she let her son use the Parlette name?"

VIII

The curiosity of the two sisters was restrained only until, in Kathleen's room, with their baggage still unpacked, they were alone with Joan. Then Kathleen seated herself on the edge of the bed and began to remove her dust-stained clothing—first her shoes and stockings, then her white shirt-waist with its high lace collar and its starched cuffs; then her skirts and under-things. Kathleen, always plump, had grown thin. She

84

got up, looked at herself in a tall mirror, said "Damn!" to some wrinkles that had definitely traced a sagging pattern over her face and neck; stared resentfully at the dolorous flabbiness of her shoulders and breasts, and returned to the edge of the bed where she sat envying Gail, who was still attractive, even if somewhat blasé, and Joan—especially Joan, who, still retaining her youthful and lissom figure and who revealed vital beauty of face and spirit, was joyously attentive and solicitous.

Kathleen said, "Well, here we are," in a jaded voice, touched with a suggestion of rancor. "Home again, to find ourselves with"—her pause was flat with futile remonstrance—"well, with a curious collection of oddities. A battered-up prize fighter, a show girl and a boy who calls himself Gregg Parlette. He might be a long-lost brother. But he isn't. Who is he, Joan?"

Joan was looking into a closet, and for an instant braced herself there to resist the shock of the sudden question. Not quite formed in her mind had been a certain impulse of sentiment, a decision to take the girls into her confidence should she feel she could depend upon their love and charity. When she felt a coldness stealing over her she knew she had hoped in vain. She faced them calmly and felt calm. She was thinking of Webster—of the advice he had given her. Webster, who had told her to lie. She said, "Gregg is my son," proudly, with a smile.

Kathleen was ready to smile cynically but held it back, so that Joan could see only the intention on her lips. Gail merely watched her. Kathleen said, "Well, that's news indeed. We didn't know you had married. Who was the lucky man?"

"Gregg's father is Frank Dade." The name was strange to her, and she did not like the sound of it.

"Your husband—of course?" said Gail, still quietly intent.

"Naturally," Joan said.

"Then why not call the boy Gregg Dade instead of Gregg Parlette?" said Kathleen.

"Preference, I suppose," Joan said. "At first I thought of him as a Dade, but later, when I saw how greatly he resembled Father and Dan, I changed my mind."

"Permanently?" This was Gail.

"I hope so."

Kathleen said, "Sounds like a separation. Was it?"

"It might be called that." She was able to smile at them. "He—Frank—was called away before Gregg was born. He hasn't come back." She felt she had to tell them the facts they might find out from others.

"That was terribly thoughtless of him," said Kathleen.

"Sounds more like desertion than separation," said Gail. "He probably ran off with another woman. Why on earth didn't you get a divorce? I wouldn't have stood for anything like that."

"Gregg is going on eleven," said Kathleen and watched Joan's face with guarded alertness. "That's what he told us. And you say his father has never seen him. Almost eleven years of waiting for a husband to come home can mean only one thing. Two, I should say.

86

You don't believe in divorce or another man hasn't appeared. Which is it, Joan?"

Joan said, "Why should it be either?" and walked to the door.

"Oh, come, Joan," Kathleen said. "We haven't seen you in an age and we are dying of curiosity to know more about your runaway husband. I hope he was handsome. But of course he must have been, to win you when you were so young. You couldn't have been quite seventeen—nearer sixteen, weren't you?"

"It was after Father died," Joan said and wondered if they had always been as they now were, or whether their experiences in the East had changed them. Were they strange, or had her own experience and her constant longing for happiness given her a new conception of life and people? Or had she forgotten what her sisters had been like? Well, whatever had happened to them or to her, they were her people and she loved them, though at this minute they aroused in her a feeling of defensive anger. What would happen if they discovered there had been no marriage? She shrank inwardly at what she saw in their faces, though she was outwardly so calm and quiet that she puzzled Kathleen, who pursed her lips and looked at Gail.

"You say it happened after Father died? That was after we left, of course," said Kathleen. "Yes, you were about sixteen, past. That's so very young for a girl to marry. It would make you almost eighteen when Gregg was born. It was too bad your husband had to leave without seeing his boy. What on earth made him do it?"

"Business—he said." Now Joan was certain about the purpose of this inquisition, and she wondered why they had not put it off until after they had changed their clothes.

"It is perfectly natural for elder sisters to discuss the marriage of a younger sister," said Gail. "Do believe in the charity of our motives, Joan."

"Of course," said Kathleen. "Don't think we are merely prying. To be sure we were astonished when your boy told us his name—Gregg Parlette. That aroused our curiosity, of course. It must have been very difficult for you to bring the boy up without a father. But I suppose the cowboys were helpful. Tom Hackett perhaps. Or Bob Webster. Webster, very likely. As kids you and Webster were obviously in love. I can see both of you now as you used to run around the ranch. Bathing and riding and sitting in dark corners. How does it come you didn't marry Webster, Joan?"

"Kathie, you are being absurd," said Gail. "Everybody knows that a girl never—well, almost never—marries a boy who grows up with her. The grass is always greener in the next pasture, you know. So are girls when they marry the handsome stranger."

"He couldn't have been handsomer than Webster," Kathleen said. "Was he, Joan?"

"It is strange that I have never noticed Bob in that way," said Joan. "I liked him for something different. I think it was for his honesty and loyalty, and because he always minded his own affairs." She hid her annoyance behind a steady sisterly smile, though Kathleen saw that the corners of her lips were white and that deep in her eyes was hot resentment. "You'll forgive our sudden interest in you, Joan," said Gail and began to strip for a bath and a change of clothing.

"Of course," said Joan quietly. "It isn't so sudden after all. I've had eleven years to prepare for it." She smiled at their startled glances and left them.

Kathleen listened to Joan's steps in the hall. Then she looked at Gail, enjoying her consternation. "I think it was Webster," she laughed.

Some of the whiteness of Joan's lips had gone when she came upon Mona in the living room, and she met the show girl's inquiring gaze with a composed smile.

Those questions had been questions of curiosity, of course. And no doubt Kathleen and Gail *were* interested in discovering what had happened to her during the eleven years of their absence. They were justifiable questions. Yet Joan knew that the spirit of curiosity may be cynical or suspicious. The loyalty and love of the remaining members of her family—now like strangers to her—were going like a glorious sunset being swallowed by the purple shadows of night, and she must steady herself to meet this new disappointment. Charitably, she thought of their weariness after the long ride from Maricopa. Perhaps they had only been irritable and would be different after a wash and a change of clothing. She said, walking to the big door opening upon the veranda, "Where are my other guests?"

Mona answered, "Bat's hanging around the horse

corral as usual. He's got a yen to ride a horse, and Gregg has already promised to teach him. Gregg's with him now. Say, Gregg's a great kid, isn't he? Looks something like you, but more like that painting of your father hanging in Webster's office. It made my ticker go pitapat when I saw how he hugged you when he rode in. It must be swell to have a boy like that. He's so big and strong that you have to look at him twice before you know he isn't a man."

"Yes," said Joan; "it is—swell, as you say," and leaned a little farther out of the doorway so she could see the boy more closely, where he sat on the top of the adobe corral fence laughing and talking with the prize fighter. She saw Paul standing near a corner of the harness shop watching the two, but all were so far away that she could not see the expressions of their faces. Still farther away she could see Webster in front of the foreman's shack. He was washing his face and the dying sunlight caught the bronze in his hair as the water splashed over his head. Gratitude for his loyalty and dismayed regret for her sisters' hard cynicism stabbed her with quick contradictory pangs as she stood there and heard Mona saying, "Don't you think it is time for me and Bat to clear out?"

Joan looked at her reprovingly. "What made you think of such a thing?"

"Your sisters. Maybe they'll think it will be crowded here from now on."

"There's plenty of room, Mona. You know that." She was apprehensive that the girl was really thinking of going. Already she had grown to like Mona and had enjoyed her personality and the slang expressions that crept into her speech. She was breezy and entertaining, even if some of her observations were somewhat pointedly shaped with the double-edged-worded barbs of her profession and her sophistication. She was frank, too, and could be depended upon to discriminate between the real and the counterfeit.

"Then you *really* don't want me to go?" she said, catching the concern in Joan's voice.

Joan said, "Of course not!" impulsively and added, "You are not offended because I changed your room, Mona? For of course Kathleen wanted her old one."

"I'm flattered," said Mona. "Why, you poor lonesome kid, I've had the time of my life here. And now I've got the room next to yours and can duck in there once in a while and weep on your shoulder—when I'm thinking of your handsome foreman. Say, he's a pippin, isn't he?"

Joan said, "Do you think so, Mona?" and understood that the show girl was only tantalizing her.

"Surest thing you know," Mona said. "I'm stuck on him to a fare-thee-well. And I think Kathleen and Gail are a little dizzy too." She saw there was no sign of jealousy in Joan's eyes, and a certain thought she had vagrantly entertained went out of her mind forever. *It wasn't Webster.* "They've hurt you, some way," she said. "You looked white around the gills when you came in here a few minutes ago. Well," she said when Joan silently turned her head away, "so far as I can see, the Parlette kids who went East with the Parlette kale didn't turn out so well."

"They were just tired and cross," Joan said. "You'll like them better when you get acquainted with them."

"You certainly are an optimist," said Mona.

Yet when, after a while, Kathleen and Gail came down the hall and merely paused in the living room, where Mona sat reading a week-old newspaper, and inspected the decorations, which were the same as when they had left the ranch to go East, ignoring Mona entirely and looking past her with arrogant disinterest, and went out to the great veranda where they dusted off the seats of two of the heaviest rockers with dainty flicks of their handkerchiefs, and sat in the chairs and gazed critically about them, at some new adobe buildings erected during their absence, and decided between themselves that the chairs on the veranda were the same chairs they had known, Mona, listening and smiling, was certain their presence would add nothing to Joan's mental comfort, and that she herself would not bother to extend herself to become better acquainted with them.

At the supper table she watched them and saw how they patronized Joan and studied Gregg's face. They completely ignored Mona and exchanged comprehending glances with Paul, and not too guardedly made verbal references to Battling Kelso's disfigured face. Kelso countered by not even looking at them. He gave all his attention to Gregg who, seated at his right, was admiringly watching him and listening to him.

". . . so he cops me on the beezer when I wasn't looking," said Kelso, continuing his recital of the final round of his fight with the champion.

"The beezer?" said Gregg, wide eyed. "What is a beezer?"

"My beak," explained the fighter. "My nose. He broke it with that wallop, a right. I hadn't learned how to duck or block them. The champ knew it. So he plants another right on my ear and made a cauliflower out of it. Then he hangs a shiner on each of my lamps and busts my kisser with a lallapalooza; and while I'm coming in, not seeing him any more, he finds the button with a haymaker and stops me cold. After that I learned to be scientific. But then it was too late. I'd slipped."

"What's that?" said Gregg.

"I'd lost my strength. My condition. My punch."

"Tom Hackett said you hit the Pilgrim awfully hard," said Gregg.

"Ten years ago hitting him like that on the back of the neck, I'd have killed him."

"You landed on the champion and didn't kill him," said Paul. "You were outclassed. The champion murdered you."

"Sure," said Kelso, smiling through his puffed lips. "I found that out."

"He was a sucker for a right," said Mona, looking at Paul. "The same as *you* were a sucker for the gamblers." She laughed, but the sting of truth in her words annoyed Kathleen, who knew of her brother's faults.

Kathleen looked past Joan and at Mona. She said,

"Paul wasn't a gambler. He was a gentleman sportsman. There is a difference, if these people were able to distinguish it."

"I'll bite," said Mona. "Where is it?"

Joan said, "Don't be so touchy, Kathie. Paul always gambled. All of us knew it. He was always gambling with the cowboys. And Father dragged him out of a Tucson gambling room."

"I'm not ashamed of it," said Paul. "All right. I'm a gambler. But Kelso never was a fighter."

Kelso smiled, holding no resentment. Joan had reproved her relatives for attempting to adopt a superior attitude toward her guests. And Gregg disliked his uncle Paul for depreciating the ability of his new-found hero.

IX

Most disturbing to Joan was her sisters' obvious lack of affection for herself and Gregg. When they noticed the boy at all it was with speculative glances which bore maliciously harbored suspicion and doubt. They had not accepted her statement of Gregg's parentage. They had not, like Mona, shown interest in him or affection for him; and Mona's "He's a great kid, isn't he?" had thrilled her and had touched chords of happiness which were muted in the presence of her sisters. Of course they must never know how their coldness was hurting her.

After supper when Mona, smiling at her, went out into the darkness of the veranda, and Paul followed

Mona, and Gregg and Kelso went to the fighter's room where the boy was to inspect the boxing gloves and perhaps take his first lesson with them, she lingered in the living room with Kathleen and Gail, dutifully to entertain them. It was like entertaining strangers to whom you are trying to be nice but who put you on the defensive by asking impertinent questions. They did not look at her at all until after they had completed a leisurely inspection of the living room. Then Kathleen said, "Joan, don't you ever get tired of looking at the same things year after year?"

"Why should I? I like everything here."

"These old decorations—the deer heads, the guns, the bearskins, the powder horns; that Indian headdress with the dirty feathers on it; the arrows, the adzed beams, those cracked panels, that beastly fireplace; the Buffalo robes and—and all the rest of the junk?"

"They were Father's. I shall always keep them." Joan wondered if Kathleen had forgotten how John Parlette prized these relics of the pioneer days.

"Bosh!" said Kathleen. "The place looks positively medieval. Like an old fort. With loopholes everywhere. And what on earth do you do with your spare time? Just sit around and mope over your lost husband, I suppose? Well, if he was mine I'd show him a thing or two."

"I always have plenty to do," said Joan and thought of days, all too short, when the work with the cattle, the garden and the accounts, kept her busy.

Kathleen was looking at some books on several open shelves. She walked to a table where still other books were piled, looked them over, and then glanced around the room. She seemed to be searching for one book in particular. She said, "I suppose Padre O'Meara is still living in the mission hacienda?"

"Yes."

"Is he as old fashioned as ever?" she asked. And when Joan told her she had never thought of the padre as being old fashioned she laughed and said, "The danger is in becoming old fashioned without knowing it. That is what is wrong with you, Joan. You are stuck in this old dump—buried here, if you only knew it—while the rest of the world whirls on its way, perhaps somewhat dizzily, but going somewhere anyway. People are having a good time, and living. Do you go to parties or dances, or take trips to the various watering places to associate with the best people—important people who do big things? You don't, of course, and because you don't, you miss the broadening influences of life."

Joan said, "It is probably exciting and interesting to people who like things of that kind. But though I like to read about big cities and their people and their activities and pleasures, I also like this country—the land and the things it grows; the cattle and the horses, and the young calves and colts toddling around on their funny long legs. I have always loved this ranch, from the first day I saw it, I think. Perhaps I inherited my love for it. Father loved it, you know. It has one virtue that endears it to me—it never changes, as people change."

"Well," said Kathleen, "I never change, if that's what

you mean. I hate this land you profess to love. I have always hated it. And I don't see how you, or anyone else, can say you love it. You don't really. The lovely things it grows are sand and rocks, and Indians trying to scalp you, and smelly horses and men, and a sun that bakes you, and snakes and other crawly things, and horny cactus that makes you think of a forgotten cemetery with headstones so hoary with age that they've grown prickers, and—" She caught herself overgoing it and added, "I certainly do hate it, don't I?"

Now Joan remembered Kathleen's shuddering at the sounds of calves bawling in the branding pens, and Gail's fits of sullen fury over nothing at all, or over trivial crosses, and Kathleen's continuing criticism of everything—the food, the dust, the sun, the distances one had to travel to towns in search of a good time; her contempt of the people she met in such towns; the way both girls had quarreled with her, and dominated her, and had ignored or repulsed her every attempt to win their affections. Padre O'Meara had termed them "Unfortunate accidents of birth" when greedily they had taken their father's money and had gone East with it to squander it, leaving Joan alone, giving her no choice. And this land which they hated had brought Joan nearly a million dollars which was safely invested. It hadn't brought her the happiness she wanted, but it had brought Gregg. And now it had brought her sisters and Paul, all of them improvident and foolish, from a world in which all of them had failed to make their way. Yet she was not dismayed by this new obligation, for she had learned to calmly discipline herself against the sardonic ironies of existence. So she was able to smile at Kathleen's vehemence, knowing that her sisters, having had the advantages provided by the social existence of their choice, had made no greater success of their lives than she had.

"You've scads of money, they tell us," said Kathleen, seeing how little her criticism had affected Joan. "And you don't have to live like a hermit. Why don't you chuck all this and go East with us? Just think of what a sensation you would create! The papers would be full of it. 'Millionaire ranch girl flees the desert! Special train bearing Western beauty arrives in New York!' Wouldn't that be exciting? Stunning gowns, theaters, swell bathing beaches, the races, receptions, balls—a life of pleasure. And men who would make you forget your handsome runaway husband."

"And a yacht," said Gail. "And the best hotels. Gregg in a good university where he would become a gentleman. What will he be here, Joan?"

Joan said, "Gregg will be what he wants to be—a ranch owner. He shall have the ranch and most of the money I have when he is twenty-one. I shouldn't like the kind of life you describe and I am sure Gregg wouldn't."

"I see," said Kathleen. "You are going to stay here and wait for Dade. You are going to martyr yourself over a foolish love affair. It's incredible!" Disappointment drew her lips into a drooping crescent. She added, with strained patience, "Don't be a fool, Joan. Why should you waste your life on *one* man?"

"You are wasting your breath, Kathleen," said Joan. She was wondering if they had always been as shallow as they now were, and if they thought they had succeeded in hiding their selfish interest in the proposed Eastern conquest. She added, "I won't even permit myself to think of leaving here—for any reason."

Kathleen dropped into one of the big horsehair chairs without taking the precaution of flecking dust, real or imaginary, from it. She sat staring at Joan, making an effort to conceal her disappointment and chagrin behind a smile of patient resignation. Gail was frankly furious. She said "Damn!" and walked to the open doorway, to see two figures she thought to be Paul and Mona sitting in the moonlight on a far edge of the veranda. Mona was laughing mockingly, and the sound seemed to carry a derisive implication of Kathleen's failure to interest Joan. Gail contemptuously shrugged her shoulders and came back into the room in time to hear Kathleen say, "That was one of the reasons we came here, Joan—to take you back with us."

Joan was now wishing they hadn't come. They were so transparently insincere. She said, "I'm sorry you have wasted your time," and went out into the kitchen and dining room where she talked briefly with the two Mexican women housekeepers—wives of Mexican gardeners—and the cook. She came back into the living room to see her sisters thumbing the pages of the family Bible, and instantly she surmised that this was what Kathleen had been looking for in her search among the books. She said, forcing calmness, "Oh, the Bible. Are you going to read a chapter, Kathleen? Father used to do that." But she knew they would not read. They were searching for the family birth record which her father had kept. Their suspicious minds would explore every possibility to discredit her, to provide them with means to again dominate her. Knowing they would find no record of Gregg's birth, she nevertheless was held there in dread fascination, looking over their shoulders as the pages were turned, wondering why she had not anticipated this search, and why, during Gregg's lifetime, she had not herself made the record. It would be embarrassing to explain the absence of such a record, and humiliating to endure the questioning their warped minds would devise. They said nothing to explain their purpose in looking through the book, but there were the beginnings of malicious smiles at the corners of their mouths, and both leaned closer as the sought-for page was disclosed. The inward stiffening which had aided Joan through the suspense became limp relief as she read at the bottom of the record—where it should be, if it was there at all:

Joan Parlette. Born April 16th, 1860.

This was in her father's crabbed handwriting. She thought it would be all. But it was not all. Following closely was:

Married June 20th, 1876, to Frank Dade.

Born of this union, Gregg Dade, July 10, 1877.

This last was not her father's writing, but she recognized it. She quietly slipped away. And while the sisters were chattering over the book she fled like a drifting shadow, though a radiant one, over the dusty yard, past the harness and blacksmith shops and the storehouse and the bunk and mess houses to where, while the sun had been setting, she had seen Bob Webster splashing water over his face in front of his adobe quarters.

He was sitting in a tilted chair near the door of the building smoking. He got up when she stopped in front of him and removed the cigarette from between his lips. He said, with a note of laughter in his voice, "So they found it first pop, just as I thought they would, after getting acquainted with them on the trip in. I had some trouble remembering the dates, and maybe they're not so accurate. But they are convincing."

Breathlessly she said, "When did you write it?" She stepped close to him, so that he saw her eyes were bright with gratitude.

"The night Brother Paul drifted in. I thought he'd be a snooper too."

"Thank you," she said and kissed him. She had to stand on the tips of her toes to do it, her lips brushing his as lightly as thistledown, and his clasping arms just missing her as she ran toward the house.

X

The half-dozen riders who had entered the planked portals of Delafan's gambling house in the Dela Plaza—changed to Ott Street by the yearning of respectable citizens of Tucson for the elimination of the old Mexican flavor and many vices—were greeted by a swirling cloud of tobacco smoke strong with the odors of whisky, garlic, red peppers from steaming con carne dispensed over a counter in a corner, and the man-smell of horsemen and freighters, Mexican and American, who wooed the siren-voiced dame of fortune at the gambling tables. The Parlette riders, in town for a spree, with the consent of Bob Webster, who permitted digressions of this sort for the sake of contentment in the outfit, were variously named Antrim, Brill, Elwell, Fanning, Gumbo and Jansen. They had visited many Mexican cantinas as well as numerous American saloons, and they grinned and blinked at the lamplights gleaming through the heavy atmosphere of this room. They wanted to play faro, and when they finally got their bearings they gravitated to the layout like moths to the flame.

There were no bets on the layout. Someone had swept the counters into a little heap on the green cloth, and the dealer's hands were idle on the dealing box. The casekeeper, lacking interest with no customers facing him, was leaning back in his chair. A swinging lamp, suspended over the faro table, shed its yellow-white beams upon the dealer whose masculine attractions were enhanced by a shirt of spotless white linen and a stock of the same material, neckband and drooping frontispiece caught together with a diamond stickpin. He exuded opulence and professional suavity as he smiled at the Parlette riders who stood in front of the layout, ready to place their bets. He said, his voice soft amid the din of rattling poker chips, the whir of roulette wheels and the shouting of betters, "Place your bets, gentlemen. The bank is ready," and pulled up the sleeves of his immaculate shirt.

"What's the limit?" said Gumbo and drew a handful of silver dollars from a pocket.

"Fifty and one hundred," said the dealer. To Gumbo, who had played faro, this meant that any amount up to the larger sum could be wagered upon one card except on the last turn, when the amount must not be larger than the lower figure.

Gumbo played, and the casekeeper deftly slid the buttons along upon their rods. The others—Jansen and Elwell duplicating Gumbo's bets—also played. Dealer and casekeeper were quiet and attentive but unconcerned while the riders won some bets, for the gamblers were running a brace game, with a set of undetectable signals, and they knew that in the end the riders would lose.

Gumbo said, after losing half a dozen bets, "Luck ain't running my way," and jingled the silver that still remained in his pocket. He drew out a handful, counted it, replaced it. He added, "If I was Joan Parlette now I'd bust your damned bank."

His belligerence seemed to amuse the dealer who sat still, his hands idle, looking at him. "Joan Parlette," he said musingly. "Seems I've heard of her. Sure. She owns that big ranch on Antelope Creek. Your boss? She's got money, you say? That's interesting." He dealt a card. The casekeeper moved a button opposite a corresponding card on his little machine, so that the players, at a glance, could tell what spots had been played or were still in the dealer's box. The stakes were small, for payday for ranch hands brought them no great riches, yet such as they were they represented months of toil and danger. The dealer raked in several pieces of silver that Jansen had placed on the king of clubs. The king would have won for Jansen if the dealer had not pulled two by the sand-tell method. He was using a straight box, with certain of the cards roughened or sandpapered slightly, so that by pressing heavily upon the top of the exposed card the one beneath would stick to its neighbor above, and he could deal the two with one motion.

Gumbo, keen eyed, had noticed the extra thickness of the card that had slid out of the box. He watched the casekeeper swiftly slide the buttons along their rods to record the extra card. It was confusingly fast work.

"You ain't been around here long," said Gumbo to the dealer. There was a hint of frost in his eyes.

"Only a few weeks. I've hardly got acquainted."

Other men were now playing. The dealer paid some bets and raked in others. He looked at Gumbo. "Her father died about eleven years ago, I hear," he said.

"Eleven or thereabouts," said Gumbo.

"There were some brothers and sisters, I understand. Where are they?"

Jansen lost another bet. Again the dealer had withdrawn two cards from the box. "You know more about them than you let on," said Gumbo. "More than a stranger should know."

"What if I do?" said the dealer. He laughed. "Don't turn your wolf loose. I used to know the Parlettes."

"Do they know you?" said Gumbo. "I've heard they are particular about who they get thick with." He watched the dealer's face grow pale, then red. He saw how the dealer accepted the insult by pretending not to hear it and by asking a question, "Any Indian trouble around?"

"Some. And getting worse. Stay close to your dealer's box. It's safer. And surer." He drew out a handful of silver dollars, counted out twenty-five and placed them on the deuce of spades, to lose. Jansen had lost again and was standing back, scowling at the layout. The other Parlette riders, their pockets nearly empty, were listening to the strange conversation. They were watching Gumbo, having caught the antagonism in his voice. He was their leader and they would support him in any action of his, whatever it should happen to be.

The dealer fingered the box. The casekeeper fiddled with the buttons but watched for the dealer's signal. It came—pull two. With deliberation the dealer shoved out two cards, their sanded surfaces clinging together so that there seemed to be only one. The deuce of spades was now the top card in the dealer's box. Gumbo had lost, having played the deuce to lose, and the deuce had won. The dealer said, "Place your bets, gentlemen," and grinned at Gumbo. The casekeeper reached for the marker buttons as Gumbo, with one sweeping motion that began at his hip and ended on the green cloth, swung the muzzle of his six-shooter down upon the case-keeper's hand, smashing it before it could reach the buttons.

"Brace game," said Gumbo and jerked the muzzle of his gun upward, so that dealer and casekeeper were looking into its dark ring. They were motionless, having also looked into Gumbo's eyes which were now flecked with hate. The casekeeper had not moved his crushed hand but was grimacing with pain and looking at a spreading rivulet of crimson spouting between the knuckles and wrist, staining the green cloth under it. The hand was his right and it was broken. All the Parlette riders were now close to the faro table and were enraged by Gumbo's accusation of trickery. Four had not drawn their guns, seeing Gumbo and Jansen would prevent retaliation. They ignored the casekeeper and watched the dealer whose face was as white as the stock around his neck, and his mouth open, as if paralyzing fear had stilled in his throat a meditated cry for help.

"Tinhorn!" said Gumbo, his voice cold with contempt. "Dip into that cashbox and fork over the two hundred you snatched from us! Fast! Or I'll perforate that dickey you're wearing around your neck. Exactly two hundred," he added as the dealer began to toss

106

silver dollars to the table top. "No more, no less." He watched the other riders transfer the money to their pockets, and again spoke to the dealer, watching his eyes, seeing the lids narrow to slits. "You've got a rattler's ideas and a polecat's liver," he said. "But you're keeping both of them where they won't poison anybody. Adios."

They were laughing as they went out of the doorway, with the crowd in the room between them and the two gamblers at the faro table whom they watched as they departed. The casekeeper was still staring at his broken hand, and the dealer's mouth was still open.

They roistered around town, doing the things they wanted to do and drinking more than they needed, as if they sought, like camels, to store against the desert's thirst. And when in the morning they compared notes and realized that by remaining longer in town they would break their word to their foreman they mounted their ponies and rode across the dry bed of the Santa Cruz into the polychromatic veil of distance, behind which lurked the dangers of their trade.

Two camps in the open brought them to a certain crossing of the Gila, where life and fertility reigned in the swales, and nondescript brush lifted leafy barriers under drooping fronds of cottonwood. The river levels were carpeted with bright green grass and the atmosphere was aromatic with the sweet smells of sage and mesquite and paloverde with its smooth glittering bark and its clusters of yellow blossoms. Then again they abruptly met the desert, corroded with the vitriolic yellow and russet brown of its repulsive verdure, and rode into it, virtuously conscious of having earned the foreman's trust.

They were dots of life in a dead land upon whose broad expanse were salient features which through constant observation and necessity they remembered; and with their ponies racking along in a Spanish chop-trot, they threaded the wilderness of space, mentally noting various landmarks by which they set their course— Three Mile Mesquite, Choya Ridge, Face Rock, Sacaton, Skull Canyon; finally sighting the peaks of the Big Horn Mountains and the towering spire of Cathedral Rock. And there, presently, wandering northward through the hills and creases of the land, they saw the ribbon road that stretched from Maricopa to the head of Bear Flat. They rode along this road for several miles, and then angled westward toward a narrow valley set between low hills. And there was the ribbon road again, meeting them near the head of the valley. They halted to scan the vacant country, and then became interested in some puffs of dust in the valley bottom at a distance.

"Cattle," said Antrim.

"Strays," said Brill speculatively.

"The Bear Flat outfit is rounding them up to haze them back," said Fanning. "Now why did they let them break out?" He had seen horsemen dropping down a hill behind the cattle.

Ground-hugging dust clouds trailed away in the wind behind the distant horses, with their riders, who were so far away that they were hardly distinguishable to the watchers above who had pulled up in a dry wash which formed the only outlet from the valley at their end. A stand of timber halfway up the wash screened them from the country below, yet an instinct of caution sent them scurrying into the further concealment of boulders and brush beside the trail, from where, with professional interest, they waited and watched.

"They ought to turn them now while they've got room," said Gumbo. "Pretty soon they'll have to ride the slopes, and they've got no horses with short legs on one side."

"Seems they ain't aiming to head them off," said Brill, scratching his head in perplexity. "They ain't showing no speed. They're trailing them."

Elwell growled, "They're just dumb, that's all. Just the other day Hackett was telling me he'd got rid of all the thickheaded hands. . . . Now the slopes are crowding in and they've lost their chance."

"They'll turn them up here where there's plenty of room," Antrim said, his voice dripping sarcasm. "They're afraid of cramping their style."

Gumbo said, "They're needing haircuts," and enjoyed the bewilderment suddenly showing on the faces of his friends who stared at him. "Your eyes ain't so good," he said gently. He pulled his rifle from its saddle scabbard, worked the drop-lever action enough to see that there was a cartridge in the firing chamber and spoke again. "They are wearing their hair in braids, decorated with feathers and wampum. One of them is showing turquoise beads."

"You mighty near had me dizzy," said Antrim. He stared at the running cattle and now saw that Indians were driving them. They were quite a distance away and heading straight for the wash where Gumbo and his friends waited. Antrim added, "Likely they're Spotted Elk's braves. There's a dozen steers. I tally six Injuns, unless some have laid back to jump any of the Bear Flat boys who might hop on their trail."

Gumbo looked at the ribbon road that circled the base of a low hill at the head of the wash, to angle away again out of sight.

"We'll jump them here," he said. "They'll be traveling slow, horses and steers being winded by the climb. If any get by, we'll pick them off as they go over the hump of the wash." His voice was low, yet it crackled with decision. No thought of mercy annoyed Gumbo. As natural enemies, the Apaches were to be massacred. So Antrim, Brill and Elwell were detailed to cross the wash, there to fade out of sight, while Fanning, Jansen and Gumbo were to stay where they were. No Apache, missed by the first blast of rifle fire, would escape by riding under the shoulder and chest of his pony.

Waiting, the men discussed their visit to Tucson, and their talk finally got around to the faro dealer. "He's bothering me," said Gumbo. "I've seen him, or a jasper like him, somewhere, sometime. Wherever it was, or whenever it was, I hated him as much as I hate him now." Not less did he hate the Apaches, now heading up

110

the wash, driving their stolen cattle ahead of them. The pleasant country, basking in the afternoon sunlight, was disturbed only by the voices of the Parlette riders, talking and laughing, and by the Parlette steers, laboring up the wash ahead of the Maricopa Apaches, riding single file in negligent fashion, exulting in their successful foray, with the folded ridges of the land rising between them and the hard-riding men of the Bear Flat outfit.

At the hump of the wash, just where the ribbon road circled the hill, the steers slowed to a scrambling, grunting walk, their foam-stained muzzles and flanks steaming from their long run. The Maricopas were crowding them when one after another the rifles of Gumbo and his friends cracked dryly from the flanking brush. Four of the Maricopas pitched off their ponies at the first fire, but two, untouched, slid under the shoulders of their animals, showing only a leg and an arm each to Antrim, Brill and Elwell, but making fair targets for Gumbo, Fanning and Jansen, who calmly riddled them, while from the brush opposite bullets thudded into the copper-hued bodies of the fallen rustlers whose twitching muscles showed them to be still alive.

The startled steers cleared the hump of the wash and went lumbering off into the higher country, while Gumbo and his friends emerged from the brush to follow them to round them up and head them back.

The red men were lying at the edge of the ribbon road near the head of the wash. Their bodies were scattered, for in their death agonies some of them had clung to their frightened ponies from which they had dropped as the animals bucked them off. On the ground of the wash were flint-tipped lances and arrows; a long bow decorated with eagle feathers; a rusted carbine which looked like a Spencer; an octagonal-barreled Sharps rifle; a powder horn and a rawhide quiver with some feathered arrow shafts sticking out of it. The scene was not so pitiful to Gumbo as it might have been if there had not always been in his mind certain memories of what Apaches had done to white men and women he had known. As it was, he was stirred to vindictive satisfaction as he dismounted, while the other riders watched from their saddles, to walk among the bodies to make certain all were dead and not able to reach their tribe with the story of the ambush.

"Hackett got two of them a couple of weeks ago," he said to the other men. "Webster was telling me just before we started for town. Four of them were after Gregg—figuring to hold him at their camp until Joan came to raise the beef ante. The kid busted Two Feathers with the barrel of his gun and—"

He looked intently at the partially visible face of an Indian who was lying stomach down with his legs drawn up as if about to spring upright. But Gumbo was certain the legs no longer had any life in them, for there was a bullet hole in the Indian's back, and though his lambent eyes were open, they seemed to be set as they stared into the dust of the wash. Gumbo said, a little surprised, "Here's Two Feathers now, with his elk's teeth biting the dust," and leaped back to slap swiftly at the holster on his leg as Two Feathers rolled over on his back and shot him in the left side with a six-shooter which had been concealed under him. Gumbo's gun kicked upward and Two Feathers' head jerked back with a hole between his malignant eyes as Gumbo steadied himself and smiled foolishly at his friends who began to run toward him and were at his side in an instant, carrying him to a flat rock upon which they placed him and tore his shirt away from the wound. Apologetically Gumbo said, "I wasn't looking for a dead Indian to move that fast." And again, a little later, "You boys round up them steers and head them back. I'll climb aboard my horse and light out for the hoodlum wagon in the flat."

"You'll do no riding for a while," said Brill. "That's a bad place to be hit in—just at the edge of the last rib. Lucky it went through." He swabbed the wound out with water from a canteen, packed it with his neckerchief to stop the bleeding and ripped off his shirt to use as a bandage. Then the five literally ripped two small saplings from the roots and rigged up two travois poles to which they lashed a blanket and placed Gumbo upon it. Gumbo heard shooting and raised his head to see Jansen and Elwell administering the coup de grace to the other Apaches. They did it vindictively, while the other riders lashed the root ends of the sapling to the saddle on Gumbo's pony.

Reaching the Parlette ranch, their holiday ending in near tragedy, they were relieved when at the mission house Padre O'Meara told them that while there was danger of complications there was little doubt that Gumbo would survive. He said, sitting beside his patient, while studying the sober anxiety on the somber faces of the others, "You had no such concern over the Apaches you killed."

They grinned. Said Antrim, "Most of them never knew what hit them. And we left their hair on."

They had brought Gumbo to the mission house because there was no doctor available, and they knew the padre would take care of him as he had taken care of many of them in similar circumstances. They had tried to avoid being seen from the ranch house, but such things are always seen, and now here were Joan and Bob Webster, listening as Jansen briefly told them of the killing of the red marauders, not neglecting to accentuate the punctuality of the return from Tucson. And a little distance away were Kathleen and Gail. They had talked to Gumbo and had seen the wound— which made Kathleen's face blanch—and now they were standing under the dangling fronds of a cotton- wood, near enough to see the padre's ascetic profile and to suddenly remember that he had always been hand- some.

Kathleen said, "I don't see why a good-looking man should bury himself in this place. I mean he would be good looking if he didn't seem half starved."

"I think he puts a little of that on," said Gail. "For effect."

"I remember that you never liked him," said Kathleen. "Do you remember why?"

"His absurd philosophy. According to him it is sinful to enjoy the good things of life. If that is so, then we are all wicked."

"I think he is more than half right," said Kathleen. "That's why sinning is so easy and why it's so hard to be good. That man Gumbo is nice looking, isn't he?"

"I like the blond one—Brill, they call him. But I heard one of them say they are part of the Gila outfit, and I suppose they'll go away as soon as they are certain about Gumbo."

Padre O'Meara went into the hacienda, leaving Gumbo on a canvas cot in a little patio, where Webster and Joan leaned over him. Gumbo's friends, reassured, sauntered to the cottonwood where they stood, hats in hand, talking with Kathleen and Gail. Gumbo had some news to communicate to Joan and Webster but was uncertain as to how best to tell it. He said tentatively, "Glad we wasn't unpunctual coming back, boss. That brush with Spotted Elk's rustlers was the only fun we had."

"That hardly sounds natural," said Webster. "Then it was quiet in Tucson?" Joan was looking at Gumbo's cheeks, into which spots of crimson had come, staining the bronze.

"Yes—quiet," he said. "The only fun we had was with a gambler." Joan noticed that Gumbo avoided her gaze and her cheeks went a little white as she remembered that Gumbo had been with the Parlette riders before Frank Dade had come—and gone.

"A gambler," said Webster and stared hard at Gumbo.

"Dealing faro," Gumbo explained.

"Dealing faro," repeated Webster. He knew Joan was watching him, that she was watching Gumbo. And he suspected she was thinking exactly what he was thinking—that Dade's letter had come from Tucson.

Webster looked at the group under the cottonwood. He was wondering if they could hear Gumbo's voice and was certain they could not.

"He was running a brace game," said Gumbo. "He was not so slick. But the casekeeper! That was a scream. He tried to look sorry when we lost."

"Of course," said Webster. "The casekeeper being sorry makes it easier for the loser. But you won once in a while?"

Gumbo nodded and smiled. "Just often enough to keep us betting. He wore a linen dickey with a diamond stickpin in it."

"The casekeeper wore a dickey?" said Webster. "If it wasn't starched it was a stock."

"It was a stock," said Gumbo. He looked at Joan and wondered why her lips had grown so white. "The dealer wore it," he said. "Slickest-looking gambler I ever saw. The kind of a man you remember—once you've seen him. I kept thinking I'd seen him before. I kept wondering *where* I'd seen him. Bothered me. Do you know why you hate a man?" he said, looking from Webster to Joan and thinking that Joan seemed to be holding her breath. "Something about him disgusts you," he said. "I hated him from the minute I clapped eyes on him.

Claimed to know you, Miss Joan, and I told him you was mighty particular about choosing folks as acquaintances. Seems he'd heard you'd got rich. Wanted to know about your brothers and sisters."

"You hated him, you say," said Webster. "Usually when Gumbo hates a man—" He hesitated and looked down at the gun on his leg.

"Not this time," said Gumbo. "I don't know *why* I didn't kill him. I had the notion. But after I smashed the casekeeper's hand and had bent my gun on the dealer, making him fork over the two hundred he'd fleeced us out of, I got softhearted, though I'd already picked out a spot on the dickey for my bullet to go into. Later I fired that bullet into Two Feathers' forehead."

"You had seen the dealer before," said Webster. "Can you remember where?" Joan was watching Gumbo's face. Padre O'Meara approached. He paused near by, not wanting to listen, yet interested.

Gumbo's brows were screwed up in an effort at concentration. "Yes," he said, "I've seen him before. In this country. I can't place him. But in another gambling joint in Tucson I inquired about him. His name is Frank Dade."

XI

It was no shock to any of them, and Gumbo's gaze, roving from one to another, could read nothing which would lead him to think that his news had any value. He thought Joan's steady, pale smile seemed a little bleak, but the changing light brought on by the flaming colors of the sunset probably was responsible for that; and her hand gently stroking his head made him wonder if the fever surging through him had not loosened his tongue and colored his thoughts.

Joan said, "I am so sorry you were hurt, Gumbo," and though he had heard of her warm sympathy for distressed man or beast, he was astonished to see that her eyes were clouded with emotion. He was uncomfortable with guilt, for until now he had only half believed the legend of her concern for the unfortunate. When he saw Webster's eyes flickering with a frosty light and caught Padre O'Meara making the sign of the cross he smiled ironically, thinking they believed he had received a death wound.

O'Meara followed Webster to the far side of the house, where they stood in the shadows of the mountains as the color flood of the sunset poured its beauty into the skies behind them. They listened and could hear Joan talking with Gumbo.

"A beautiful and wonderful girl," said the padre. "She has great courage. Not a sign or a sound out of her." Webster's quietness amazed him, too, yet looking back over the years he could not remember when the foreman's emotions could easily be read.

"She's seen many wounded men," said Webster and strode away. He came back instantly and stared hard at the padre. "Damn it!" he said, "say what you mean! Don't talk double to me!"

"I never have," said the padre. "Straight talk is in my

mind. It's you. You don't want to believe it—that Frank Dade is coming back."

Webster was breathing hard. The padre considered this phenomenon. The man still loved her—had continued to love her throughout the years. That was why no other woman had ever been able to hold him—it was why he had been quietly taciturn and coldly civil in respecting Joan's decision about the gambler.

"So you know," said Webster. "You have known all along!"

"Of course. Do you think I have no eyes? Listen, son. You loved her when you were both children. Before Frank Dade came. She always hung around you. You taught her to ride, to shoot, to swim, to rope and to brand. Maybe you were too young to know that you might have married her in those days. That was not your fault. Youth thinks there is plenty of time. You couldn't foresee that Dade would come to carry her off her feet. I remember that while Dade was here courting her, after his fashion, you were away on the range earning your spurs. And when you came back Dade was gone. And after Gregg came you avoided her."

He was startled to learn that the padre knew how it had been between Joan and him—that his neglect of her had been noticeable. Yet it hadn't been altogether neglect. He had thought she had wanted time to adjust herself to Dade's desertion. He hadn't wanted to appear to force himself upon her. He felt sick inside, thinking of how he had missed his chance to win her. And now all at once he saw that the fault had been with him and not with her. That as the male he should have been the pursuer, the aggressor, as the males of all species are aggressors, following nature's scheme in that respect. By his timidity or reserve—or because of a stubbornness which made him feel he should have been invited—eleven years of his life had been wasted. Had he thought of her merely as a woman he would have taken advantage of Dade's absence. Then she might have forgotten Dade. Then, perhaps, there might have been a son of his own. But she was not merely a woman, to him. More than a woman. It was curious about his feelings for her. The woman in her, of course, yet something more than womanhood. Nothing that he could put a finger on, to hold it down for examination. The way she had of holding herself erect—fearlessly; a way she had of looking at you, doubting. A breathless worship of her beautiful hair, wavy and brown, with bronze ringlets in it and unruly wisps that added a reckless and abandoned glint to the meditative calmness of her brave, steady eyes. He had always thought he would have liked her as well if she had only been his sister. He walked to a corner of the house and looked at her leaning over Gumbo, talking to him, stroking his head, and thought of her doing that to Dade—thought of more intimate things the two of them had done. The bitter jealousy in him made him tingle with rage, so that when he strode around the corner of the house and stood beside Gumbo, and drew Joan away, his face was white, even though he spoke with husky steadiness, knowing Joan was curiously watching him. "I'm pleased with you, Gumbo."

Gumbo stared at him, wondering why he should be pleased. Pleased that he hadn't killed Dade? He said, "Thank you, boss," and looked at Joan, whose face was as pale as Webster's. Gumbo studied the fading light as he listened to Joan and the foreman walking away—heard them call "so long" to himself and the padre. "I've seen him more pleased," he said. And then to the padre, who had approached, "Was it the light that made him look like that?" and watched the padre's face, which was pallid and solemnly wistful, as he traced the riders growing dimmer in his sight. The padre thought of the big gun on the foreman's thigh and crossed himself. His lips moved. He walked slowly away without answering Gumbo.

"I couldn't face them now," said Joan, thinking of the family, and turned her horse from the dry arroyo that led to the creek road. Wondering what her feelings really were, Webster rode beside her through the wooded country north of the ranch house and followed her when the trail narrowed in the thick-growing brush of the shallow valleys. The poison of jealousy turning his blood to water, fanning his stomach to physical sickness, an ineffable yearning swelling his lungs as he stole glances at her when she rode beside him or watched the graceful outlines of her figure swaying ahead of him. He did not speak when at the crest of a low hill she drew her horse down and slid from the saddle.

She leaned lightly against the shoulder of her horse, a faint wind stirring the recreant, tantalizing wisps of hair at the nape of her neck. Her head was erect, her face and throat outlined in the faint paleness of the twilight, softly defining the nobility of the profile he loved— suggesting her character. Waiting for her to speak, he sat astride his horse watching her. To make it less awkward for her he got down and pretended to tighten a cinch buckle. Then he rested his arms on the saddle and wondered why he did not step over and put his arms around her. He wanted to, in spite of his jealousy of Dade. But first she had to show him that she wanted him. Some sign must come from her—some invitation. He would not throw himself at her. He would not stand up like a dog and beg for her love. The kind of love he wanted from her was not the kind of love Frank Dade had taken.

He was astonished when she said calmly, "So he is coming back. Back—at last."

"Did Gumbo say that?" he said and saw her smile wryly.

"He told Gumbo he had heard that I had grown wealthy. Hearing about my money was what brought the family back. It will bring him back too."

"If that's what he wants," he said.

"What else could he want?" she said and faced him, her eyes bright with rage.

"You," he said and saw her wince.

A grimace was stiff on her lips as she said, "You don't believe that! It isn't sense, is it? He's had eleven years to think it over. The same as my sisters and Paul. What brought them back? Money. They came back as soon as they heard I had money. He came back too."

It wasn't like her to be cynical. Yet it was a good sign, and it made his blood surge with vindictive joy. He said, "You seem to be sure of that."

"Wouldn't it bring you back?" she said. "Or any man?"

"I'd want the woman," he said. "If it was you and me. The money wouldn't be interesting."

"Oh, it wouldn't!" she said. "Aren't all men interested in money?"

"What will money buy?" he said. "Not you. What good would it be to me then?" He was eager, seeing her eyes widen. "Suppose money is bringing him back?" he said. "That's what *he* is thinking about. It's what you are thinking about. That's important. You don't have to take him back if you don't want to." He was trying not to make the mistake of condemning Dade but he added, "You've got to figure out why he left you."

"Wouldn't you have left me?" she said, watching him. Her chin was high, defiant.

"A baby coming wouldn't scare me out of the country," he said. "A man ought to be able to face his responsibilities."

"Aren't all men—just men?" she said, derisively calm.

So that was what her experience had done to her— destroyed her faith in men. Even with Dade staying away it would be difficult to win her. She had made his words about responsibility sound foolish to him. Before he could think more about it she said, "I shouldn't have said that. You always were a man. You and Tom Hackett. If it hadn't been for you and Tom—" Her voice choked, and he knew she was remembering the coming of Gregg. Now he was remembering, and pitying her. Remembering her bravery, her uncomplaining silence through the years. It made him hate Dade more intensely.

"I don't blame you," he said. "It wasn't exactly fun. Or any fun remembering."

She tossed her head as if she were throwing something bitter out of her mouth, and he interpreted the gesture as indicating that she would never again taste that certain thing. Yes, it was going to be difficult. And now he knew why there had never been any invitation.

But how was it to be with Dade? Dade would come back. What would his reception be? He remembered her agitation upon receiving the letter from Tucson which he had delivered to her. How she had been ready to go to Dade, the station wagon ready, with her bags piled into it, and old Miguel waiting. She had not gone to Dade but she had been thinking of going. How near had she been to taking the second bitter taste? That was the question which had been bothering him, which he was now considering as he watched her.

He said, "You've changed since a month ago when I brought you his letter. You were ready to go to him."

"I knew that was what you thought," she said and laughed nervously at his blank look. "That was why you slapped your boot that day with your hat. That was funny. It was why you called Dade 'tinhorn.' I could read your thoughts that day." She looked at him, her head held sideways, apprehensively, for she could see the black jealousy in him.

"Could you read *his* thoughts?" he said and felt a savage joy to see the pain in her eyes. "His thoughts were not always clear to you. You didn't fool him but you fooled me. Only I didn't know it. Yes, I showed you what I was thinking about that day. I brought you his letter. I brought in the Gila outfit to escort you in case Spotted Elk should have notions. Your bags were in the station wagon. Old Miguel was ready. Yes, you could read my thoughts. They showed you I wanted you to do what you wanted to do."

"Maybe that was the trouble with you—with us," she said. She was thinking of their boy-and-girl relationship before the coming of Dade—of how she had ruled him. "You always let me have my way," she said. "That made me headstrong and wild." In the deepening darkness he saw her chin go up again. She sighed and said, "Oh, Bob, don't ever change! Always show a woman what you are thinking—any woman you love. Never keep her guessing."

Now that darkness was between them her voice seemed steadier. He looked around and saw the twilight shutting the world out from them, from her and himself, and there came to him the sudden thought that perhaps she had led him to this place to settle things between them. Her words, "Don't ever change. Always show a woman what you are thinking," seemed to prove that the invitation he had longed for had finally come. Her voice had been meltingly soft, even in its steadiness.

He said, with a dry huskiness that came from years of repressed emotion unleashed in this wild moment of possible fulfillment, "I think you have always known what my thoughts are, honey." He had feared this moment would never come, though he had dreamed of it many nights when his hopes had been high. He moved toward her, thrilled by his own eagerness, considering the phenomenon of his shaking muscles and the ecstasy in his swelling lungs. She had turned from him and was facing her horse, and she said "Oh!" in astonishment when she felt him close behind her; and she put her hands against his chest and tried to hold him off when he seized her and turned her around to face him, crushing her against him so tightly that their bodies might have been one. He could not be gentle with her with this madness surging through him; and though she cried out that he was hurting her, he drew her closer than ever and kissed her again and again, smothering her cries which he thought were only protests against his eagerness, holding her lips with his own in spite of her efforts to escape him; and at last when she succeeded and buried her face in his shoulder, still helplessly struggling, frightened at the now tender fury of his emotions, he kissed the tantalizing wisps at her temples and the nape of her neck. Then, holding her still, she fighting to free herself, he laughed. "There," he said, "that's what I think." His voice was still husky, and there was a ring of triumph in it, a great sigh of ecstasy. Now he became conscious of her struggles, and he took hold of her shoulders and pushed her back a little, trying to see her face; heard her saying in a voice which was bitter cold with rage and shame, "You— you—oh!" over and over, until he began to remember that she had not responded to his passion, and released her, standing there trying to see her, now understanding that he had made a mistake in thinking she had invited him.

She retreated and from the darkness spoke to him. Her voice was quivering with angry scorn. "So *you* think I am like that too?" she said.

"Like what?" he said. "What's wrong? Is it a sin to tell a woman you love her? If that is so, I have sinned since I began knowing you."

There was a queer mixture of dismay and misery in her derisive laugh.

"You're thinking of him," he said.

"Yes," she said, her voice muffled between gasping breaths. "Of course. *You* didn't think of him. He's my husband, isn't he? You told me such marriages as the one we made are common in this country. You made a record of it in the Bible. Now you think—*what* do you think?" she said.

She had misunderstood his passion, and he was now farther away from her than ever. "That you've got your morals mixed," he said. "That you don't know your own mind. You still love him."

"No, no, no!" she almost shouted. "I don't!"

"Keep a man guessing," he said. "Keep him blundering along. He feels more natural that way."

"Oh, you don't understand!" she said.

"What?"

"That I don't love him. I thought you would know, without talking about it, that I had no intention of going to him that day just to be with him. That was all over—long ago. Over and done with!" She stomped furiously upon the hard earth of the hilltop. "I—I hate him! But I feel I am married to him. For years I've hated him. I've hated myself. But I was going to him for Gregg's sake—so Gregg would have a father. So that he could hold his head up. I thought you would know—that you did know. At least after you told me ours was a marriage—and I didn't go to him. Men don't understand. They never understand. And I hate all of them. I hate you—too!"

She must have been climbing into the saddle while she had been talking, for she jumped the horse past him and was gone into the darkness before he could reach his own mount to try to intercept her. He could trace the increasing distance between her and himself by the diminishing sounds of hoofbeats that carried to him.

XII

His thoughts lucid as the pale dawn, he sat on the edge of the bed and pulled his nightshirt over his head. Naked, he tested the chill of the breeze that drifted in through the open doors and windows of his shack. The

128

padre had been right about Gumbo. The padre had a way of putting his finger on things. Right now, after a week, Gumbo was riding south to the Gila with the men who had shared his vacation in Tucson. Gail and Kathleen would miss Gumbo.

Over the top of the corral fence the hills were rising out of the ghostly and unnatural light, their crests tinged with deepening and glowing pink against the fading purple of the mists at their bases. In his bare feet he walked to a side wall and took a gray flannel shirt from a wooden peg. He dropped the shirt to the top of the bed, pulled on his socks and trousers, drew his belt tight and stepped into his boots. Returning from the watering trough under the windmill with a pail of water, he splashed some into a basin and washed his face while thinking of Joan. And now his thoughts were not so clear.

The woolen shirt made his flesh crawl but its warmth was pleasant. He understood what Joan had been getting at. How she felt. Her experience with Dade had made her disgusted with all men. She thought they were all alike. Well, most of them were alike. But he should have known right away that she had sought an ideal and had been disillusioned. He would have known if his hate for Dade had been less strong. He hadn't been able to feel anything else. His hate had clouded things. She had made it plain that she hated Dade. That's what she thought right now. How would it be, later, after she had seen him? It wasn't clear how she was to keep Dade from claiming her as his wife when he returned, as he would, to discover he was married to her. There was the record in the family Bible to confirm his claim, and the record had already been read by the family. And suppose she didn't hate Dade after all? Suppose what she thought to be hate should turn out to be something else?

Breakfast was early at the mess house, but nobody was up yet, so he stood in the front doorway of the shack and greeted the emptiness far and near with contemplative interest. Fringing the gardens near Antelope Creek was a grove of paloverde and mesquite and alder. Nearer the creek were some willows and cedar and spruce. Behind some cottonwoods reared the fluted barrels of the saguaro. Spanish dagger blossoms fluttered their snowy white amid the vivid yellow of paloverde flowers and the bell-like blooms of the yucca dangling from their tall center rods. Stretching into the levels around the creek were broad acres of green garden truck. Horses in the corrals were beginning to nicker inquiringly; smoke from half a dozen chimneys above adobe shacks began to trail wisps of acrid wood smoke into the clear atmosphere. He scanned the country, feeling that a change had come, but began to realize that the change was in himself, that it had been brought by a grim question that was engaging him, which he could not decide. Should he kill the gambler?

He saddled and bridled his top horse and rode to the padre's hacienda where he found the padre in his garden dipping water from a barrel and sprinkling it upon some scraggly annuals seared by the sun. The thirsty sand gulped the water avidly, and the padre greeted him with a doleful smile. "It is hard to bring beauty to this country," he said. He added, "Gumbo rode yesterday with his friends."

"He reported to me before he left," said Webster, adding, "It's easy to bring hell to this country."

The padre perceived the grimness in his visitor. "Violence is in your mind, my friend," he said. "Don't! She is honest with herself. With you, with everybody. Let her decide. I saw this in your face last week. Killing him wouldn't settle anything. It might make things worse between you and Joan."

"How in hell do you figure that?" he said. Intolerance of all interference stirred his shoulders, showed in strange cold flecks in his eyes. The padre thought of a striking rattler.

He said, "Gregg is his son. Gregg loves you. Do your thinking before you meet Dade. There is always an afterward, and nothing is so empty as regret. Do you think Gregg would continue to love you if you do what you have in mind?"

He hadn't thought of that. It had looked simple. A bullet crashing into the gambler, ending a problem. Life would go on from there. But would it? A stealthy apprehension crept through him. He would be hurting the kid! His hate would become a double-edged weapon, harming the innocent. He felt a new respect for O'Meara, a dealer in reason and forethought. But hate was still bitter in his stomach. It stormed through him. He said, "Blazes! He'd know nothing about it. He needn't be told."

"He would see it in his mother's eyes," said the padre. "She would tell him someday, when she herself had grown to hate you. Then you would hate yourself."

He knew what hate was—there were eleven years of it in him. Also, there were eleven years of knowledge in the padre's mind—the knowledge that Gregg was Dade's son. Joan had told him, of course. He might have guessed it. So that was the source from which Joan had drawn her courage and her patience!

"How do we know what thoughts men harbor?" said the padre. "Or women? Do we know what emotion may next possess us? You are Joan's friend. Would she want her friend to kill a man she once loved—still loves perhaps? How do you know what her thoughts are?"

"You are fluent with your questions," said Webster. "Does a man lie still when he sees a rattler about to strike?"

"You'll do no good lying to yourself, my friend. Murder is murder. Have you thought of what Kathleen and Gail, and Paul, would think if you were to kill Joan's husband? You made a record of the marriage, you know."

"She has told you everything," he said. "Even how I doctored the record."

"The same night. And asked me to bless you for it. A sacrilege. I can see now that you didn't deserve to be blessed. But you won't kill Dade." Here was a man he loved. He had watched him grow. It was a hard, grim country, and to survive it man himself had to be hard. But the foreman was a fair fighter. "The one thing I have always admired is courage," he said. "Joan has it. You have it. Doing things is not always as right as not doing them."

Indecision rode back to the shack with him, and his mind revolved the padre's philosophy, "Doing things is not always as right as not doing them." It was integrated with *courage,* which the padre admired, and with *honesty,* which was in Joan's character. But it jangled with the hate in his heart, and with the knowledge that Dade was an evil element in his life and Joan's, like the poisonous loco or the quicksands of the bottoms. The things he knew were fixtures—the hills, the plains, the cattle, the Parlette riders, the Apaches, the sand and the dust, the heat-scorched verdure and the eternal sunlight. Elements of harmony because they belonged in the scheme of things. All adjusted to the inexorable rules of nature. Fit to survive. Yet Dade was to survive. He was not fit but he represented complications. Was there a fault in the padre's reasoning? Should he provoke Dade to an act of aggression that would justify killing him? He thought, "The padre would know I was sidestepping the complications. Joan wouldn't be fooled."

Eastward he saw the rose tints of dawn advancing in nebulous waves. Behind him streamers and lances of red and gold touched the mountaintops and splashed seas of silvery pink over their shoulders. In the glowing tide eastward appeared a horseman riding slowly over the Bear Flat road. He passed the ranch house, and the clip-clop of hoofs on the hard shale near the stable brought a stableman out to meet the horseman in front of the foreman's shack, and an instant later he was greeting Joe Lathrop, buyer for Brock & Lee, who had arrived earlier in the season than usual.

Lathrop had breakfasted with Tom Hackett's outfit in Bear Flat, but after his horse had been put away he went to the mess house with the foreman and gave him news of the sections of the country he had visited. "Dry season," he concluded. "Low-grade stock. The Parlette steers are the best I've seen. Nothing to make you top lofty, though. You're just lucky to have some grass and water—and a boss who knows her business."

Lathrop's sixty years, with more than a quarter of a century of them spent in the saddle, had ripened him, bowed his legs and laid a sheath of leather-like skin over his face which was a raw bronze with rivulet wrinkles running to genial confluences around moonlike eyes, limpid sly with wisdom and knowledge of life. "By George, my wife likes your boss, Miss Joan," he said. "I made a mistake bringing her here last year. Danged if she didn't want to come again this trip." He chuckled. "Had to draw the line on that," he added. "Too much poker playing to take proper care of a wife. And she ain't exactly gentle when left alone too much. Mistakes," he ruminated. "We all make them." He winced. "I made a mistake in Maricopa. I got too friendly with a stranger. He tagged onto me as soon as he heard I was coming here. I'd had a few drinks and was kind of loose with my talk. A slick looker. Wore broadcloth, linen shirt and a stock with a diamond in it. Name of Dade. Said he was a friend of the family and was coming here for a visit. He'd been hanging out in Tucson. Hinted maybe he'd stay here for a while. Said he was a particular friend of Miss Joan." He stared hard at Webster and caught his breath. "What in thunder have I been doing now?" he said.

"You've been playing you're a kid wearing diapers. With an arrow," said the foreman. He shoved back his chair. "Known as Cupid," he said. This had to come now since the family knew it, but he had not expected it to come through Lathrop. He stared at his half-finished breakfast, surprised that he no longer wanted it. He got to his feet and looked at the buyer's face, crinkled in dolorous, dismayed inquiry. He explained, "You've brought her husband back," and maliciously enjoyed the buyer's consternation, who yelled, "I didn't even know she was married!"

Webster thought, "Her husband doesn't know it either," and said, "If you'd known he was her husband you'd have done well to let the Apaches get him."

"So that's what you think of him!" said the buyer. He scratched his head. His sly eyes rolled. "You don't sound overly enthusiastic about him," he said. "He was scared of that."

"That I don't like him?" said Webster. "Could he tell it that far away?"

"Scared of Apaches," said the buyer. "His hair was standing on end. Coming through the hills I thought he'd try to crawl into his horse. Rounding a bend at the head of a valley a few miles from Bear Flat, we came upon some Maricopas that somebody had blasted hell out of, and this here Dade man turned green. He bolted, yelling. I found him hiding in a rock pocket, shaking like he had the ague. Gentlemen, hush! He had hysterics. 'Don't let them take me!' he yelled. He like to have died of fright."

"Likes to run away from things," said Webster. "He ran away from Joan." He hitched at his gun belt. "The Maricopas you saw were killed by Gumbo and his friends coming back from Tucson. The Maricopas had cut out a few steers from Tom Hackett's herd, and Gumbo and the boys wiped them out."

"Hackett told me," said Lathrop. He moved to get a better look at Webster's eyes. He sucked in a deep breath. "Why did he run away from Joan? What kind of a man would run from a woman like her?" he said.

"Some men don't like to walk the floor nights with a baby," said Webster.

"That was Gregg," said Lathrop. "Why, sure! My wife thought it was funny that his name should be Parlette when he called Miss Joan 'Mother.' " He batted his eyes. "So Dade is his father!" he said.

"Being Joan's husband is more important," said Webster. "Remember that."

"Oh, sure." Lathrop tried to be casual. "But I still don't see—"

"Only two people are seeing," said Webster. "Joan and him." He walked to a window and looked down the Bear Flat road where heat devils were already dancing.

"Keep guessing," he said to the buyer. "Keep blundering along. The clearer things seem to you, the less you know about them. If you know only cattle you don't have any problems. Did he say when he would ride in?"

"Oh, Dade, you mean! No. You see, I forgot to tell you. Hackett sent word to you that he couldn't bear to see Dade leave him too suddenly. So he is prevailing upon him to stay with the outfit until you get there."

"Thank you," he said. "It was bothering me some. Hackett isn't always so hospitable and thoughtful."

He took the buyer to his shack and permitted him to select one of the two beds. Ready to go out, he looked at the buyer. "She is kind of soured on Cupids," he said. "So you'd be wasting your breath." He grinned to take the sting out of his words.

"She's got a capable foreman," said Lathrop.

"You're almost as direct as she is," said Webster. He tied a gray neckerchief around his throat. "In some things," he said.

He went across to the stable and mounted his top horse. From a window Lathrop watched him ride to the ranch house, where he dismounted, tied the animal to an iron ring at the veranda edge and entered his office. Lathrop whispered to the world at large, "They don't make them any deeper than that man. She'd be lost without him. I wonder if she knows that?"

XIII

There was a sound from the open door at Webster's
back and he turned from the desk and saw Joan
standing just inside the door, watching him.

"Hello," he said and turned back to the desk.

"Hello," she said. She coughed nervously. "I heard
you come in," she added.

"I tried to be quiet," he said; "I didn't want to arouse
the family. I didn't think you would be up."

"I always get up early," she said. "You know that."

"Yes," he said; "that's right."

"You rode over to Padre O'Meara's place," she
said.

"Yes."

"Did you see him?"

"Yes."

"What was he doing?" she said and smiled at the
floor.

"Watering his garden," he said. So this was to be the
way? Matter-of-fact, as if nothing had happened
between them a week ago. Well, then, this was the way
it was to be.

She said, "Joe Lathrop is here. I saw him riding past.
He is early this year, isn't he?"

"Is he?" He kept her waiting until he was certain
impatience would disturb her calmness. Just like in the
old days. "Why, that's right, isn't it?" he said judicially.
"If he's here, he's early."

"Don't try to pretend," she said. "I saw you go into the mess house with him."

Without turning he said, "Then why did you ask me?"

"To see if you would be as rude as you were in the old days."

So *she* was thinking of the old days! He said, "The old days, eh? And what did you decide?"

"That there has been no change in you. A month ago, when we talked in this office, I thought you had changed. You seemed almost like a stranger to me. I couldn't understand it then, but now I realize it was because we hadn't seen much of each other in eleven years. You are still the same Bob Webster. Not very different—I think. You are still stubborn, and violent and impetuous."

"All right. We agree on that. I haven't changed. We all change. So I am trailing behind. What of it?"

"Nothing—only—" She became silent. He turned in his chair and saw her biting her lips. Her eyes were perplexed. "Nothing, of course," she said. "But it seems so strange—the way things happen. Something happens to us as the years go by. What is it? Do our characters change? Or do our experiences harden us? Or make us wiser? Or does our sense of values change? What is it? Everything seems different!"

"We just grow cynical," he said. "We do a little thinking before we do any jumping." He looked straight at her, knowing she was thinking of Dade and himself. "We do more guessing," he said. "And we don't guess wrong so often."

"I see," she said. "You are reminding me that I guessed wrong—at least once."

"Twice," he said. "The first time didn't count because you hadn't known men very well. The second time will count because you know men better." He was hurting her, for he saw her wince. He would not throw himself at her again, and if he saw that she still loved Dade he wouldn't hang around and cry for the moon. Right now she felt she was married to the gambler, and she had resented his proffered love because it had seemed to her like faithlessness or physical passion. The padre was right—she was honest. Hunger for her was strong in him. It made his voice husky with jealous regret.

"You have to know," he said. "Dade is here."

"Here!" she said. "Now!" She plucked at the collar of her wrapper, then dropped her hands in front of her and twined the fingers together. Her face was colorless, and she was trying to be calm, but he saw her writhing fingers and was certain she was writhing inwardly. What her emotions were he could not guess, but he could see the agony of frightened indecision in her widened eyes and in the pallor of her face.

"Not here—now," he soothed. "He's in Bear Flat with Tom Hackett. Tom didn't want him to bust in here suddenly."

"Tom didn't want him to come?" she said and stared at him in disbelief. "You didn't! You're going there— now! I've been wondering why you looked—seemed— so queer! What are you going to do to him?"

"That's what I'd like to know," he said and leaned

back in his chair and held his chin in a cupped left hand, while his right thumb hooked his cartridge belt. "I've been trying to decide. Would he be more valuable to this country as boss of the Parlette range, or as something you could mourn over when you feel a mourning fit coming on? He's yours, you know. You'll have to do the deciding. Do you want my personal inclinations? They are mighty violent."

"Oh," she said, "I don't want him—killed!" She stared hard at him, trying to solve the riddle of his pretended indifference. "I hate him," she said, "but not enough to have that happen to him. I'd hate you, too," she added, "if you did it!" and he mentally scored another for the padre. "I'd hate Tom Hackett—much as I love him—if he did it. Tell him that, please!"

"Tom will do what you want him to do," he said. "I'll see to that." He got up and went to the door, she moving aside to let him pass, looking at his shoulders and the back of his head as he stood for a moment in the doorway, she thinking of that night a week ago and holding her breath as she remembered one wild instant in which she had almost responded to his passion. When he turned and faced her she was trembling, and he thought it was because of her concern over what might happen to Dade.

"Let's get this straight between us," he said. "I love you. I have loved you since we were kids playing together. What happened a week ago wasn't the kind of thing you thought it was. In spite of what happened between you and him, in spite of what I told you about marriages and what I wrote in the family Bible, you are still Joan Parlette, and not married. Maybe you have different ideas about it. The family will have different ideas, and so will Dade." She saw a white line stain the bronze around his mouth and knew strong emotion was tugging at him. "I had ideas too," he said, and she saw the white sweep entirely over his face. "Dreams," he said. "Of you and me. Of Gregg being *my* son!" He laughed in self-derision. "Well, I guessed wrong too."

She was breathing fast, blinking at him. Her face was whiter than his, and her lips were set tightly together. "I didn't know," she said, whispering. "I never knew. I— I thought—us being together so much"—she caught her breath—"that we would never grow up, I suppose." She gave him a slight pale smile and her eyes questioned him. "Was that why you seemed so strange to me—the day you thought I was going to him?"

"You'll have to answer that one," he said. "You were never strange to me." He stepped backward, toward the veranda edge where his horse was tied. He was strange to her! Would he still have been strange if Dade had never appeared at the ranch? "It is strange that we got everything wrong," he said. "And nothing right." He bowed to her and saw her watching him as if holding her breath. "I'll be gentle with him," he said. "I'll bring him the moon—the moon I wanted."

XIV

Where a month or so ago there had been California poppies there were now the wrecks of them; and the green sheen which had covered the land like a vivid mist had become the corroded yellow and russet brown of desert verdure scorched by the sun; and a spiraling dust cloud trailed him through the great flat toward the chuck wagon and the camp located far south of the ridge road leading to the spot where the wagons had picked up Mona Wilsden and Battling Kelso on their way to the ranch. He followed the snakelike doublings of Antelope Creek past groups of cattle searching for new green shoots in the bunch grass, noting their shrinking flanks and their restlessness.

"Nothing to be top lofty about," were Joe Lathrop's words about cattle in general in the country, but he found he was applying them to the relations between Joan and himself. "Let a man go to patting himself on the back and some woman will take it out of him," he thought. And, "Somewhere around the right woman would be waiting." Joan was the *right* woman, but he was the *wrong* man. Riders waved to him or shouted greetings, and he answered them or halted to talk with them. Half a mile from the camp Tom Hackett rode out of a sand draw and rode beside him, meditatively chewing tobacco. A quarter of a mile from camp Hackett spat at a clump of pale yellow flowers on a saguaro, glanced sideways at the foreman and said,

"Lathrop got here early." They reached a shallow and Webster rode into the creek to water his horse. Hackett pulled up near him and gave him a full glance.

"I'm saving the Duke for you," he said. "I'm *that* considerate."

"The Duke?" said Webster. "I thought Lathrop said Dade was here!"

"Sure. The Duke is a title he goes by in Tucson—and other points," Hackett said. "A handle he came by in his profession on account of the clothes he wears. He's a top-hand gambler. The boys heard it in town."

"You been herding him here long?" said Webster.

"Two days," said Hackett. He screwed his brows together and searched the foreman's face. "Why?" he said.

"You've lost your chance," said Webster. He jerked the horse's head up, abruptly forbidding him to drink more.

"What chance?" said Hackett. He stared hard at Webster. "To shoot him, you mean? I told you I was saving him for you. It was you he spoiled things for."

Webster urged his horse out of the water and Hackett rode beside him, eager, curious. "She don't want him killed," said Webster. He dropped the reins to the saddle horn, found tobacco and papers and rolled a cigarette. "She'd be desolated," he said.

"What's that? If the padre had educated you more, you could talk English."

"She'd feel alone," said Webster. "She hates him but she wants him to stay in this world so she can keep thinking about him."

"Hell and blazes! What would John Parlette say?"

"That we are fools to try to straighten things out for a woman," said Webster.

They pulled up in a grove of trees near the chuck wagon. A deep dark pool in the creek looked inviting, and after Webster dismounted and tied his horse to the front wheel of the wagon he undressed and plunged into the water. Hackett followed him and for half an hour they disported themselves. The adobe mud of the sloping bank was marked with the prints of bare feet where some of the Parlette riders had entered and left the water. The hoodlum wagon was standing in a clearing near the chuck wagon. The horses of the remuda were farther down the creek in a rope corral. Some shirts and other garments were hanging limp and damp from the lower branches of trees, and among them was one that drew the foreman's attention.

"A bib and tucker," he said. He stood up in the water, hip deep, glistening rivulets dropping from the skin of his shoulders and chest, white and smooth below the bronze which ran upward from the base of his neck.

"There's hell in you today," said Hackett, watching him. "But the Duke ain't no puling infant. Carries a derringer in his pants pocket. I hear he has used it. Look again and you'll see that the bib and tucker is a stock. He washed it this morning. It's dry now. Wears a diamond in it. Carries a brush to clean his clothes with and to push back his hair with. His boots are in the hoodlum wagon with him. He keeps them glistening. Wears peg-leg pants and white linen shirts. Carries a knife in a sheath under his belt, inside the pants. There's times when you can see the haft of it. He's in the wagon now, having his beauty sleep."

After Webster dressed he went to the rear of the hoodlum wagon and looked into it through the open flaps. Hackett stood near him, attentive.

"Come out and get into your pants and boots," said Webster. "I'm riding with you to the ranch house."

The figure of a man stirred and sat up. He peered out at the foreman, and they exchanged glances. He was of uncertain age, and handsome in spite of sleep wrinkles and perspiration. His tousled hair would make him look dangerously reckless to a woman. Behind his steady gray eyes were the depth and hardness of the cold-nerved man. But Webster remembered Lathrop's story of the man's fright upon seeing the dead Maricopas, and Gumbo's tale of how, facing Gumbo's gun, he had given up the money he had unfairly taken from him and his friends.

The wagon flaps were drawn from the inside. The occupant's voice came out, muffled, petulant, "Who are you?"

Webster walked away without answering. He stood at the edge of the pool and stared into it. The water was no blacker than his rage. Hackett answered for him. He said, "That's Webster," and wondered if he could make it happen right now. There was a chance. He said, "Come out on the prod—raring. Don't let him bluff you. He ain't so much of a hell-warmer."

Dade was dressing. Hackett heard him pull on his boots—the heels scraping the floor. "What *is* he?" Dade said through the closed flaps.

"The Parlette foreman," said Hackett. "He don't like the cut of your mug. Likes to order folks around. If he goes to making a pass at you, pull that pepperbox you've got in your pants pocket. He wears his gun for scenery." He whispered, "Fan that pepperbox the minute you get your feet on the ground." *If he did so, Hackett would shoot him, and it would be all over. The motive would be obvious.*

XV

Watching Webster and Dade ride away, Hackett's mouth was drooping with disappointment. Nothing had happened. Webster had not lingered to wait for the gambler to dress but had ridden away to look at the grass on the slopes. When he returned Dade was ready to travel, and one look at the heavy gun on the foreman's leg had convinced him that the derringer in his trousers pocket should stay there.

The foreman had his hate well in hand, for he could look straight at the gambler with formal politeness, as befitted his role of escort to the stranger in a strange land who depended upon him for guidance and safety. Reluctant and suspicious, remembering Hackett's advice, the gambler rode behind Webster through the flat, certain that the foreman's saturnine face was a mask for meditated violence. He was puzzled when they met riders who grinned at the foreman or greeted him jovially, but he remembered how the Parlette riders had grinned at him after smashing the casekeeper's hand in Delafan's place in Tucson. The Parlette riders were a hard crew, he had heard, and though the stake was high, he wondered if he had been wise in coming here. A thought, unformed and unexpressed until now, became definite, "Cowboys in town and cowboys in the open are different. Diffident and awkward in town, they are a potential menace of lurking violence in their own habitat." Suppose they had heard of how he had treated their boss, Joan? But he felt safe enough. He might have ridden to the ranch house alone, except that the Apaches were on the warpath, Hackett had told him. Hackett had told him that he had sent word to Joan by Joe Lathrop and she would send someone to escort him. She had sent the foreman. So he still had some power over her.

At a shallow in the creek about five miles from the camp the foreman rode into a stream to water his horse, and Dade's animal eagerly followed. Most of the cattle were bunched along the bases of rimming hills south-ward, though there were still some scattered bands ranging along the doublings of the creek east and west. Uncomfortable with a scorching sun beating down upon the back of his neck, and drenched with flinty though feathery alkali dust from a miniature whirlwind that collapsed upon him as his horse drank, Dade said, "Whew! What a hell of a country!"

Webster did not look at him. He said, "Was that why

you left it when you were here before?" He jerked the reins and spoke to the horse under him. "You'll be getting yourself a bellyache," he said. "Being a hog." He now looked at Dade and nodded his head at the gambler's horse. "Get him out of here—he'll founder himself." He looked at Dade's heels. "No spurs, of course," he said and lashed Dade's horse with his quirt. He watched the animal try to buck the gambler off, but his disappointment did not show on his face, and he rode on again, not looking back at his companion.

Dade rode closer. "How did you know I had been here before?" he said. "Did Joan tell you?"

"You're curious, eh?" said Webster. He spurred his horse ahead and rode along, humming a tune in monotone.

Dade rode beside him again. He said, "That was about eleven years ago. When I was here before, I mean."

"About eleven," said Webster. "So you've been keeping track?"

"I haven't kept track of you," said Dade. "I don't remember you."

"At that time you weren't looking for *men*," said Webster. He rolled a cigarette, his horse smoothly racking. After lighting the cigarette, he dropped back a little so that Dade was a little ahead of him. "Do you remember that?" he said. "Women were more interesting."

"Women are interesting to any man," said Dade. He began to wonder how much this sardonic rider knew about his relations with Joan.

"Sure," Webster said. "And they keep on being interesting. A man keeps thinking about them. Even being away from one for eleven years won't stop a man from doing *some* thinking. But how much? And what kind of thinking?"

"That's none of your damned business!" said Dade. He was suddenly cold with rage. This was a trap, and he had foolishly ridden into it. Back there a little ways his thoughts about the menace of cowboys in the open had been a presentiment. This man knew about his intimacy with Joan. "I see," he said. "She sent you out here to pump me! Perhaps to murder me!" He thought of what Hackett had said about this man and fumbled at the right-hand pocket of his trousers, but jerked his hand away when the foreman's voice, like the lash of a whip, snapped in his ears.

"Quit that! That pepperbox in your pants pocket will work only when a man's back is turned. Toss it into that sage behind you! The knife too," he added and watched the weapons as they flashed, momentarily, in the sunlight, to land in the sagebrush. Dade was now desperately calm. He expected to be shot, and waited to see the foreman's right hand descend to the big gun on his thigh.

But Webster rode along, now beside Dade again. "What kind of thinking?" he said, resuming his talk. "If you were to be killed, Hackett would have done it. He wanted to. Maybe you'll keep on living. Depends upon your thinking. And Hackett's patience." He touched a spur to the horse's belly. "Let's get along," he said. "She knows you are here and she'll likely want to see what kind of a critter you turned out to be. She'll probably be disappointed."

Dade now rode more confidently. Since he was not to be murdered, the outlook was not so bad. He said, "Did she send for me?"

"What makes you think she would?" said Webster.

Dade laughed. "Oh, women will remember a man," he said. "You know how they are."

"How are they?"

"They always remember a man they have loved."

Webster winced. "She loved you—you say? That's only one side of it. How about you?" He dropped back in order to see Dade's face.

"I suppose I loved her. I thought I did."

"You didn't know? How *does* a man know when he loves a woman?" He turned his head, not wanting the gambler to see the hate and jealousy in his eyes. "By sneaking off when he learns he's got her into trouble?" he said. He saw Dade's face suddenly redden, then turn pale.

He laughed nervously. "So she was telling the truth after all," he said.

"Did you think she was trying to scare you into marrying her?" said Webster. "What were you thinking about when you took her to that fake parson and told her he was the real thing?" He watched Dade shoot an apprehensive glance at him, watched him squirm in the saddle. "The truth is nearly eleven years old," he said.

151

"He's more of a man than you are. He doesn't know his father is a sneaking polecat. His mother hasn't told him."

Dade thought, "So that is what I'm running into! But if she has stopped loving me, why is this man taking me to her? This man is jealous. She wants to see me. He would kill me but has orders not to. So she knows he is jealous. She has a son who is nearly eleven, and she hasn't told him I am his father. So she has been expecting me to come back to her. The second conquest will be easier than the first."

"She has told you about me," he said. "Are you a particular friend of hers?"

Webster held his temper which sent a wave of white into his face. Since the beginning of this trip he had resolved that Gregg's first look at his father should reveal him as nature had made him, and not as he might be, disfigured by a vengeance long meditated. To smash a fist into Dade's face would be to betray the jealousy he must conquer if he was to continue to think clearly. Clear thinking might win in the end for him, with both Joan and Gregg. He said, "You're not as thickheaded as I thought you were. You have figured out that you are to be brought in undamaged. So I won't smash you up, as I ought to. You'll look like a human being when Joan and the boy see you."

"Thanks," smiled Dade. He was now still more confident. Certainly, if Joan wanted to see him, she would want to see him as he had been years ago. The foreman was jealous but he was not a fool. No doubt there was a limit to his patience and self-control. Still, now that he was safe, he could venture to express his suspicions about the man. He said, "Now that we understand each other, let me tell you that I don't blame you for wanting to step into my boots. But I suppose you found they didn't fit?"

"I think you'll die in them," said Webster. "That is, if you don't love yourself to death." He spurred ahead but presently dropped back again. "I don't want to talk to you any more than I have to," he said. "But there's one thing I've got to tell you. Put a check strap on your mouth when you get to the ranch house, or you'll die so damned sudden that you'll think the world is standing on end. Her folks are here from the East—her sisters, Kathleen and Gail, and her brother Paul. And her son Gregg is there, and some visitors. They think you were married to Joan before you left her, before the boy was born. She has told them so, and I have made a record in the family Bible to prove it. You were married by a Campbellite parson. You are to play up to that. Do you understand?" Dade nodded, his face blank with astonishment. Webster watched him and his hate became savage. "Give Joan's hand away," he said, "and I'll jam your damned boots down your throat!" He spurred on again, Dade following closely, for the ranch house was in sight. Dade saw some people on the veranda and flecked some dust from his boots.

XVI

Webster was riding ahead when they reached the veranda where the sisters and Paul and Mona were seated in comfortable chairs. Joe Lathrop was sitting on the stone floor at the veranda edge, his feet dangling, and Joan was standing in the doorway of the foreman's office. Webster waved a hand to the people on the veranda, and to Lathrop, as he dismounted and tied his horse to a hitch ring. He stepped to the veranda floor and went straight to Joan, who retreated as he approached her and met him just inside the door, where she could not be seen by the others, or by Dade, who was just dismounting. Thinking they could still see her, Webster shoved his big shoulders in front of her to block their view and to keep them from suspecting her pallor had been brought on by her recognition of the visitor. He saw how her eyes were blazing brightly with hate and shame. Stiff with shock, even though she had expected Dade to come and had been dreading the inevitable meeting with him, she did not resist when Webster lifted her lightly and carried her to a far corner of the office and placed her into a chair, her back to the door.

"We've got to see that your relatives don't enjoy this meeting too much," he said.

She said, "Thank you, Bob," and sat trembling, listening, staring brightly at him, wondering about his cynicism. "That's right—isn't it?" she said, trying to laugh, suddenly feeling like laughing, but failing to do so. "They *would* enjoy me, wouldn't they? If I made a mistake? Or if they suspected?"

"So they won't," he said. "You're busy. With some reports I brought in. Too busy to rush out and greet the returning husband. Let them think *that* over. Him too. Do you feel like rushing out to him?"

She smiled with singular bleakness. She said, "I don't. It's strange feeling the way I do. I mean I don't have any feeling at all for him. I don't care. It's like I never knew him."

Elation surged through him, but he kept it out of his voice and eyes. "He's changed, I think," he said.

"Yes—hasn't he! I only got one good look at him, but he doesn't seem the same. He *isn't* the same. Perhaps that accounts for it—for the way I feel about him. He looks gross and arrogant. When I knew him—before— he was—" She put both hands to her eyes, covering them. She was trying to visualize the Frank Dade of long ago. She did not succeed and dropped her hands from her eyes to look at Webster in sudden gratitude. "Thank God Gregg doesn't look like him!" she said. Color began to stain her cheeks, and a laugh of bitter mirth seemed to express her feelings about Dade. She said, "I've been afraid—afraid of myself. Afraid of what I might do—would do—when he came. Now I know. Thank you for giving me time to think." She lightly touched her hair here and there, tucked in some stray wisps at the temples and stood erect, smiling confidently. "I'm going out to face them, Bob," she said, and the next instant was at the door, serene as the faintly blue sky shimmering over the baked and shriveled land.

Webster followed her to the door and stood there. Though Dade had dismounted, he had not been greeted by any of the people on the veranda, for none except Lathrop knew him. He was at ease, though, and confident, knowing that things were going right for him. He knew he looked well and that he was undergoing critical inspection. He lounged toward the cattle buyer and spoke to him. Webster saw Joan smiling as she talked with her sisters and Paul, who had surrounded her. He had not seen her look at Dade. He leaned against a doorjamb and saw Gregg and Kelso riding in. Though huge, the prize fighter had become a fairly good rider. Gregg and Kelso halted momentarily in front of the stable and then rode toward the veranda.

Webster heard Kathleen say, "Why, Joan, you are perfectly radiant! And you are always so pale! What on earth has happened to you?" He did not hear Joan's low reply but read the epithet "Cat" on Mona Wilsden's silent lips as she sat in a chair watching.

Dade was also watching—studying Joan. Webster had seen stock buyers look at mares that way. Mona had been watching Dade. Her smile was a study in contempt.

Webster was not interested in the others. He was wondering how Joan would handle this situation, so full of potential danger to her pride. Then he saw her turn and look at Lathrop, who still talked with Dade. She looked past Dade and at Lathrop, and her dazzling smile stirred

Webster to malicious joy. "Joe Lathrop," she said, "you still haven't told me why you didn't bring your wonderful wife along on this trip!"

The buyer bowed to her. He said, "I wanted to, Miss Joan. But I had heard that the Apaches were around." He cocked an eye at the gambler, remembering the dead Maricopas.

Joan was now looking at Dade. His seductive smile was a failure, for she said with quiet coldness that made Mona smile delightedly, "So you have come back, Frank? After eleven years!" She turned from him and smiled brightly at the others. "My husband," she said.

Kathleen and Gail exchanged startled glances. Paul, who had been listening attentively, suddenly stiffened. Mona smiled into a hand. Webster watched Dade and saw rage in his eyes.

"Your husband!" said Kathleen. She gave Dade a critical, appraising stare and looked suspiciously at Joan. She whispered, low, again looking at the gambler, "I must say you have a very curious way of greeting your returned husband! It is like saying that someone has brought in another steer. And he is very good looking. In your place—with Gregg around—I should want to hold onto him."

"Clinch with him, Joan," said Mona. "Don't keep the family in suspense."

"I think I begin to understand why he left you," said Gail. She looked at Mona. "And why this person remains here," she added.

"He is romantic," whispered Kathleen, loud enough

157

for Dade to hear. She lowered her voice. "A little soiled and shopworn, I think, though," she added. "I can see why you didn't worry about him. I should say his mouth is a little sensuous. I don't like his eyes at all. What do you think of him, Paul?"

"Tinhorn," said Paul. "Every gambling joint in the East has one of him."

Paul was enjoying himself. He thought Joan's indifference to the presence of her long-absent husband was rather too quiet to be sincere. He added, "Still, he's back here and he has his rights as a husband. With Joan feeling the way she seems to feel, it will be interesting to see how she passes out those rights. Call him over and let the family pass judgment upon him, Joan." And without waiting for her consent he strode to where Dade and Lathrop were talking, their backs to the group on the veranda. For Dade had deliberately turned, having heard most of Kathleen's criticism of him.

"Look here, Dade, don't be so confounded bashful," said Paul. "The family wants to look you over. I'm Paul Parlette. Kathleen and Gail—they are Joan's sisters, you know—want to meet you. Surprise to us, you see. We didn't know Joan was married until she broke the news when we got here." He shook Dade's hand and Dade stepped upon the veranda and exchanged appraising glances with him. Because he thought the action would annoy Joan, Paul slapped Dade's back with an open hand and shoved him toward his sisters.

"So you are Joan's husband," said Kathleen and shook hands with him. "You are certainly welcome.

Sometimes a husband is a convenience." She thought her first impression to be erroneous, for he was really handsome, once you looked closely at him, even if there was a certain sly boldness in his eyes, which made you think he was wondering how gullible you might be. That thought, though, had come to her because he was a gambler—and gamblers were always sly and nervy. And she liked bold men. Why, he really had a wonderful personality. She thought she knew why Joan had married him. Ten years ago he must have been really fascinating.

"That seems to be the layout," he said.

"Seems to be?" said Kathleen. "But you *are* her husband—aren't you?"

"Depends on the draw," said Dade. "I mean my reception is conditional upon what my—my wife has been thinking for eleven years."

"How could you stay away from her that long?" said Gail.

"It's a long story," said Dade.

"Give him time," said Mona. "This is so sudden."

Paul gave Mona a wise smile and introduced Dade to her. "Mona Wilsden," he said. "A show girl who wasn't born yesterday. A visitor. She brought a friend with her—Battling Kelso. The heavyweight pug who fought the champion."

Dade's gaze lingered upon Mona, and Kathleen said, "Visitors have a place, even though some of them are not aware of it."

"And some of us have sisters," said Mona and winked

at Dade. She went to meet Battling Kelso and Gregg, who were sitting in their saddles at the veranda edge, wondering what had happened. Joan reached Gregg first and leaned over him, petting him. Webster was still in the doorway of the foreman's office. He thought Dade had conducted himself wisely—so far. He was tingling with admiration over Joan's masterful handling of Dade. Now he was interested in Gregg, who was aware of the subdued excitement in Joan's manner toward him and was puzzled about it, for he was screwing his brows together as he watched her. Joan, knowing the family better than she had ever known them, was certain they doubted her story of the marriage. She had heard Kathleen say to Dade, "But you are her husband—aren't you?"

Gregg's a dead ringer for Joan, thought Webster. "Oh, you beautiful kid!" said Mona worshipfully, squeezing as close to him as she could get, with Joan laughing at her. Webster saw Battling Kelso's puffed lips curve into a gentle smile as his eyes caressed the boy. He loves the kid, thought Webster. Everybody loves him. And no wonder. A little man!

"Is anything wrong, Mother?" said Gregg. His voice had a low register for his age, indicating advanced adolescence, but the peach bloom of health and youth, the clear, inquiring eyes, guileless and brave, and the satin smoothness of his skin were unmistakably a boy's.

"There's nothing wrong, dear," said Joan. "Things are rather right—at last." I wonder if that's true? thought Webster. She said it straight enough. She coaxed Gregg off the horse. "A surprise for you," she said. "Come over here with me, dear."

"I'm going riding with Mr. Kelso," said Gregg.

"You'll wait for him, won't you, Mr. Kelso?" said Joan.

"Sure thing. Go ahead, son. Your ma wouldn't fool you," said Kelso and looked uncomfortable when Joan reddened. She wasn't fooling Gregg—much. Only enough to fool the family.

Gregg slid out of the saddle to the veranda and advanced to Joan's side. She led him to where Dade and the sisters and Paul were standing. It seemed strange to her to be saying this, but she managed it calmly, with an anxious and apologetic smile at the boy. She said, "Gregg, this is your father," and wondered that she had the courage to do it.

Gregg backed away, his eyes critical, searching, doubtful, and at last—as Dade smirked with the intentness of his curiosity—resentfully. Then he stood his ground and said defiantly, "Are you my father?"

"Why, of course," said Kathleen. "There isn't any doubt of *that,* is there?" and looked at Joan.

Harpies! thought Webster. The lugs! thought Kelso. The insult whitened Joan's lips, but she held herself steady and pretended not to hear. She grew sick and weak with revulsion when Dade answered smoothly and smilingly, "Certainly I'm your father, my lad," and extended a hand to Gregg, who looked defiantly at him and stood very erect and rigid, and then glanced accusingly at his mother who quaked inwardly but gave him

161

a reassuring smile which he doubtfully returned and looked at Dade again. Amused, watching Joan, Dade thought, "Things are still going very well. No fuss so far. She's glad I'm here to take the blame for this young man. She's scared the kid won't like me. I'll make a play for him." The boy was a stranger to Dade, who was interested in him merely as an exhibit of his eleven-years-ago romance. All that the situation required of him was that he should make an effort to be the father the boy thought he should be. But he was acting a part for which his intentions had not prepared him. He was a father, though he had never learned to be one. He was amused but not impressed by this responsibility, and could not simulate sincerity with sufficient cleverness to fool the boy who had lived and camped and played and worked with the men of the outfit—especially with Webster.

Disappointed, Gregg was polite. Frank and brave, he would not play hypocrite. He said "Hello" obediently and touched the tips of Dade's fingers. Instantly he backed away, smiled apologetically at his mother, said, "So long" to all of them, turned and mounted his horse, which Kelso was holding for him, and rode away with the fighter.

"He's shy—isn't he?" said Kathleen, looking at Dade.

"He'll know me better—later," said Dade.

"Smart kid!" thought Mona. "But in her place I'd have given him a different father!" She looked at Webster.

XVII

Webster's waiting there in the doorway had done him little good. It was a thing in which he could not interfere. It reminded him of what had gone on between Joan and Dade years ago, about which he had not known enough to interfere, and of the years between, when he had been uncertain about her. Uncertain still, wanting to help her straighten it all out but barred from participation by his alien position, he was forced to stand by and listen as their tongues flayed her.

Watching the kid ride away with the fighter, he was pleased to see that Gregg didn't like the gambler. His gaze moved swiftly from Gregg to Joan, and he saw her sway a little and put both hands to her eyes, covering them. Ready to leap toward her, he caught the doorjamb and steadied himself there as she dropped her hands and looked straight at him, her eyes filled with the brightness of bitterness, her lips in a little twisted smile. Her smile grew and softened to the silent inquiry of his darkened, anxious look. It seemed to caress him with its knowledge of his concern.

The family and Dade had left her near the center of the veranda and were standing in a group at the far end, away from the door of the foreman's office. Paul had an arm over Dade's shoulder and was saying, "Old man, you'll have to take that kid in hand. He's damned impertinent." Kathleen was watching Joan while whispering to Gail, whose smile was maliciously reflective;

163

and Dade was listening to Paul while trying to catch the eye of Mona, whose face was a mask as she watched Joan.

It was dismay that had sent Joan's hands to cover her eyes, but she could not overcome it that easily. Shock over the knowledge that she could not expect charity or sympathy or understanding or affection from the family had made her physically sick. Pity for Gregg in his disappointment tortured her, and she hated the family and Dade so thoroughly that she could not speak another word to them or listen to them. Trying to seem indifferent to their glances and their talk, she crossed the veranda and went into the living room, seeking temporary escape. Just inside the door, where the comparative gloom of the big room clouded her vision after the white glare outside, she almost collided with Webster, who had stepped out of his office through an inside door.

She said, "Oh, Bob, wasn't it horrible?" and laughed harshly.

"Quit that!" he said sharply. His hands went to her shoulders, and he shook her a little. Then he held her tightly and said, "You showed them how a thoroughbred takes things." And more gently, "I was proud of you."

"Thank you," she said and raised one hand so that it rested upon his, on her shoulder. He started, peered at her in the dim light and tried to seize the hand. He meant it as a comforting gesture, but she quickly drew it away and put both hands against his chest.

"Don't," she said. "Please don't," and started to cry.

"There, there," he said, choking with rage and pity, feeling awkward and futile.

"That's like old times," she said, trying to laugh but crying instead. "Like when I used to lose my temper over things and you'd soothe me out of it." She looked up at him with plaintive wistfulness. "I wish they were back again," she said. "That *we* could go back to them. Never, never!"

"Do you wish that?" he said. "Me—too. Damn their mangy hides!" He added, "Say the word and I'll run the whole kaboodle off the ranch!"

"No," she said. "One doesn't do that to one's family."

"Him then," he said. "Dade!"

"He'd tell them the truth," she said dismally. "They'd know. And I couldn't stand *that!*"

"They're doing a lot of suspecting," he said. "That's just as bad."

"No, no. It isn't. I'll get them away. Don't you see? I don't want them to know—ever, for certain. Suspicions don't prove it. They need money. That's what they came out here for. Today—tomorrow—when I can talk to them again, I'll give them what they want. Don't do anything, please!"

"How about him—Dade?" he said. "You heard what Paul told him? About taking Gregg in hand? He'll try it. If he lays a hand on the kid—"

"Wait!" she said. Her voice was a tight whisper. "Mona's coming!" Her hands, pushing against his chest while they had been talking, had also been tugging at his heart, making him tremble. Now the fingers gripped hard at his shirt, and she shook him with desperate earnestness. "Promise you'll wait!" she said. "Promise! Wait until I have time to think!"

"Sure," he said and saw Mona coming through the front door from the veranda. Joan slipped past him and went through the living room and down the hall. Mona came near and looked at him.

"Where's Joan?" she said. "Holy gee! I'd like to scratch their eyes out!" She walked back and forth in front of him. "Cats!" she said, reminding him of one spitting. "Jeez! You'd think that all they know about a man is that he wears pants! And you—you big chump! Why don't you go out there and knock Dade's block off? The way he looked at that wonderful kid!" For an instant he thought she was about to hoot at him. But she only said "Jeez!" again and went past him down the hall.

Joan let herself into the well room, lifting the wooden bar that held the door tightly closed, locking the door from the inside with an iron hook and a staple her father had made. She would not forget the day he had made it, at a forge just outside the house, before the blacksmith shop had been built. He had been making a number of hooks for various purposes, and she had been fascinated by the white-hot glowing of the iron and by the sparks that flew from between the face of the hammer and the anvil. She thought of her father each time she entered the well room and she would never forget him. She would be a long time forgetting this day, too, she thought as she sat on one of the stone ledges in the room near the edge of the deep stone-lined well shaft.

The light in the room was opaque, for the one high window was insufficient, and the sun never came through it. Damp from the moss in the various nooks and crevices, the atmosphere was dank and musty, and sad with age. The supplies on the shelves and ledges were indistinct and the boxes and barrels were vaguely defined or formless, though a filtering light from the lone window shimmered faintly down upon rows of glasses and jars of jellies and jams that lined the walls above the ledges. It was cool in the room, and the subdued quiet of its isolation was a kind of comfort. So she sat there, away from her tormentors.

When she heard a soft tapping at the door she did not answer it. When the sound came again she said impatiently, "Who is it?"

"It's me," said Mona.

"What do you want?"

"I want you, of course, you poor kid! Open up! I want to cry with you."

"I'm not crying," said Joan, trying to keep her voice steady.

"Well, if you're laughing, I want to laugh too. I want to do whatever you're doing. That's how I feel."

Joan opened the door and stood in it. Mona entered, closed the door, hooked it and threw her arms around Joan. "There," she said; "have it out and you'll feel better. I'd cry, too, but I'm too damned mad!" She patted Joan's shoulders, her cheeks, smoothed her hair, kissed her. She said, "You've got one swell family! Nit! Eliza running from the hounds had a better chance than they're giving you! Do you want me to sic Bat on them?" And when Joan gasped, "No, no!" she said, "Let him work on Dade anyway, kid. And Paul. He'd knock them for a lopsided loop and they'd roll away cockeyed! They've got it coming!"

Joan said, "Treating them that way wouldn't stop them from thinking—what they think." She felt more calm now. And she was thinking calmly. And more clearly than she had been able to think in many years. She drew away from Mona and sat down on the ledge again, drying her eyes and leaning back against another and higher ledge. Mona came over and sat beside her, hugging her, saying nothing. In eleven years, except for Hackett and Webster, she had had no word of sympathy. And no one, except Padre O'Meara, to confide in. And here was Mona, almost a stranger, petting her, trying to console her, defending her against the acrimonious tongues of her relatives and rapturously admiring Gregg.

"They were born that way," said Mona. "Nobody knows why. Maybe they just growed, like Topsy." She hugged Joan tighter. "Are you sure you all had the same mother?" she said.

"Of course."

Mona said, "Nobody would ever guess it. It's a good thing your parents didn't live to see what *mugs* they turned out to be."

She wasn't paying much attention to Mona's chattering. She was thinking that there was no use trying to deceive the family further. Their suspicions were strong and their thoughts had a critical and cynical trend. That was their nature and they couldn't help it. There was no way to change their characters. She had to accept them as they were, and bear with them, or not accept them and tell them to go away. But whatever she did, they would still suspect. She had been victimized by Dade. Nothing could change that now. Yet she had hoped they would believe in her innocence. Instead they had begun to voice their suspicions before she had a chance to explain.

The past came out of the dimness of memory and she reviewed it. Yet it was not so clear. She could not recall what Dade had looked like in those days, or how he had won her. As long as he had been away she had been able to see him, though not clearly, but now that he was here she knew he was not the same as he had been. There came over her a feeling of guilt—as if there had been two men. She could not explain it, but she knew it could never be Dade again and that the family would never be the same to her. She was cold to all of them, cold and logical, and free.

She heard Mona saying, "What in the devil did you ever see in Dade?" and was astonished that she could think of him only as he was today.

She answered truthfully, "I don't know." Mona said, "For the love of Mike! Then why did you marry him?"

Joan said calmly, "You may as well know it. The family knows. And Dade. If the family doesn't actually know, they suspect it. And Dade will tell them. I'm not really married to him. The justice of the peace wasn't real."

She braced herself for a wild exclamation from Mona. It did not come. Instead the show girl said softly, "You poor kid," and hugged her tightly.

Mona said, after a while, "You were *more* of a kid then. A green kid. He flattered you and told you he was crazy about you. And afterward you discovered you were the one who was crazy. You trusted him."

"Of course," said Joan.

"You bet," said Mona. "You fell for him. Ninety-nine out of a hundred fall the same way. Then he ran out on you. Sure he did—the cheap skate!" She became silent. Then she said harshly, "Now he's back. After eleven years! He must have a rind like an elephant! What does he want?"

"Money, I suppose," said Joan. "He was in Tucson and heard that I had some."

"So he's back in search of the Holy Kale!" said Mona. "And he'll try to work the old gag. He'll be sick with love and a bum bank balance. So you'll come across."

"No!" said Joan. "I hate him!"

"Suppose he squeals to the dames?" said Mona.

"Let him. It's funny. An hour ago I was scared. Now I don't care."

"So *that's* it," Mona said and was so still and quiet that Joan thought she had finished and wondered what her thoughts were.

"What kind of a hairpin is Webster?" Mona said. She had definitely not finished.

"Hairpin?" said Joan.

"Crooked or straight?" said Mona.

"Oh—straight. He's been my foreman for eleven years."

"The candy kid, eh?"

"What do you mean?"

"Sweet. Reliable. A sucker for a dame. For you."

"I'd have been lost without him," said Joan. "He made what money I have."

"No woman could be lost with him around," said Mona. "He's got a pair of disturbing lamps."

"Lamps? Oh yes. You mean eyes."

"So you noticed them? I noticed them too. In that rock pocket, at Bear Flat, where I was undressed. He isn't the bashful kind either." She laughed. "Kidded me about the roll of bills I had in my stocking. Called the roll a 'spavin.' Remember, I told you about it when I got here." She sighed. "That seems to be eleven years ago too. He said he was glad he found me—undressed. He said, sizing me up, 'I'm not used to seeing so much beauty all in one day. That makes this scene rare. But ladies with spavins are even more rare.' Rare, eh?" she said. "Looks like the women have been giving your foreman the run-around. Or doesn't he go for skirts?"

"I—I don't know," said Joan, wondering if he did.

Mona glanced at her and tapped a foot on the stone floor. "I understand he was raised with you," she said. "That you ran around with him as a kid. And the padre

171

educated both of you. Webster taught you all you know about cows and horses and Indians and riding and shooting—and so on. And now you don't know whether or not he ever looked at a woman. Did he ever blush when he looked at you? Or get dreamy eyed? Or mope around like a sick calf?"

"Why, he has always been—just Webster," said Joan.

"That's what I thought. He's been around when you wanted him. When you didn't want him he'd be some-where else. When Dade copped you out from under his nose he stayed away from you. Sneaked into his den like a growly bear and licked his wounds and kept his trap shut. There's a good many men like that, and they're usually the kind to tie to. And you didn't get wise! That's rich. Can't you see he's batty about you?" She laughed derisively. "I'd have grabbed him off myself if I hadn't seen that," she said and laughed again. "I don't know why I didn't. Maybe I couldn't have got him. But that's what brought me here. I saw him with the wagon train, and when I did the world began to turn the wrong way. I'm still a little dizzy to tell you the truth, and if you don't want him I'll trim my sails a little and tack onto him." The faint light from the lone window seemed to shine on Mona's face as she said that. It made her look disturbingly beau-tiful to Joan, who caught her breath and became very still.

XVIII

She had to pass Webster's shack the second morning following and he was not in it. The doors and windows were wide open and she could see clear through into the dun dry country beyond. She had not seen Webster yesterday but had been told that he had gone with the buyer to the Gila range to look at the cattle. Her glance through the shack had been swift, yet she could see that the beds had not been slept in. He and Lathrop would require two or three days for the trip to the Gila; but while she was in the bedroom of the Estrella cabin helping Mrs. Estrella care for Marquito, who was only three, and very sick with a fever and a rash, she heard Webster's voice as he rode by. She ran to the door and saw him heading toward the big stable, Gumbo riding beside him. Half an hour later when she had got Marquito comfortable and had smiled away Mrs. Estrella's gratitude, and had been reminded again and again that she was an angel, she met Webster and Gumbo in front of the foreman's shack where they were sitting on the doorstep. They got up as she reached them and Gumbo saw the surprise in her eyes.

He said, "That bullet wound ain't quite healed yet, ma'am. Maybe I started riding before I should have started. Webster thought I had better ride in and let the padre have a look at it." He looked at the foreman and jerked his head toward Joan. "I'd better go see him right now," he said and walked stiffly away.

She called after him with instant concern, "Let me know what the padre says about it, Gumbo!" and looked at Webster, who was watching her. He said, "The Estrella kid again, eh? It's always one of them, or a half-dozen. Those oiler kids are always sick. Or their mothers. If they'd keep their shacks hoed out now, you wouldn't have to be spending most of your time nursing them. You ought to be a doctor. You're pretty near one now." He moved around to get a better look at her face, seeing a new and resolute calmness in it. Something is settled, he thought and wondered what it was.

In the small horse corral he saw Gregg and Kelso throwing a loop at a snubbing post. They were taking turns. Gregg was throwing the loop true; Kelso was missing. He called to them and they turned and looked inquiringly at him. He said, "If you'd start it lower you'd have better luck," and looked at Joan. "Gumbo was hurt worse than he thought he was," he said. "Worse than the padre thought." He couldn't solve the riddle of her calmness. Had she made peace with Dade? he wondered.

Gregg shouted to him, laughing, "Mr. Kelso says he can't throw a low rope. Says he's muscle bound. I've told him a horse will dodge a high loop, and he says he doesn't want to rope horses anyway."

Webster waved at Gregg, grinning, and studied Joan's face. "Have you managed your guests?" he said and saw that she was looking at him with glowing interest, as if she had not seen him in a long time. "You are worrying about something," she said. "Is it about Gumbo?"

He said, "How can you tell?" He saw Paul walking toward the small horse corral to watch Gregg and Kelso.

"Your eyes," she said and wondered why she had never noticed how attractive he really was. She could see why he had impressed Mona.

"They were always full of you—if that's what's wrong with them," he said. "So you managed them. How?"

"By not listening to their talk. By ignoring them." She thought, "It is true that we don't half appreciate people who are always around us—that outsiders see more in them than we do. I haven't appreciated him. Mona has."

"You didn't ignore *him?*" he said. "Your husband!" and saw a wry smile twist her lips.

"He isn't my husband!" she said and stood rigid. "What you told me about our marriage isn't true. There's got to be intention. And there wasn't any intention toward marriage on his part, even though he said so. I don't feel married to him. I—I thought I did until—until I saw him, the day he rode in with you. I hate him more than ever!"

So *that* was what she had settled. "Well," he said, tingling inside but keeping the satisfaction out of his eyes, "it's a thing everybody ought to be serious about. You can't go jumping from one intention to another. A couple of weeks ago—I mean on the day the boys brought Gumbo to the padre—you said you felt married to him." He was amazed to see a tide of crimson sweeping into her cheeks. He had never seen her like this—so calm one minute and so obviously disturbed and hesitant, and so softly vehement the next. "Intention's got a lot to do with everything," he said and felt a twinge of jealousy about certain things she hadn't told him. "His intentions. They'd be the same as they have always been."

"I haven't seen him alone. I told you I had avoided him." She was pale again, and her eyes were shadowed with resentment. "*That's* what you are worrying about!" she said.

"No," he said and saw a disbelieving smile twist her lips. "That's *your* business."

"Men are all alike," she said, sighing. "Mona gave him his room," she added wearily.

"Mona?" he said. "Didn't she think it was odd that you didn't?"

She gave him a pale little smile. "No," she said; "I told Mona that I had never married him."

"That certainly showed *your* intentions," he said.

Her eyes blinked rapidly and grew bright with sudden hate. Her throat tightened. "Ah!" she said. "You don't trust me!"

"I don't trust *him,*" he said. No, he thought, she had never acted like this before! He turned and saw Kathleen and Gail standing on the edge of the veranda of the ranch house, and Dade standing on the ground in front of them, the sun making a bright splotch of his white linen shirt and the diamond in his stock glittering. Gail was wearing one of Joan's riding suits—a brown tweed

176

with flaring hips. A Mexican stableman was bringing up a pony for her and, after mounting, she rode straight toward Joan and himself; and he thought of how, during the week of Gumbo's convalescence, before he had ridden away to the Gila with the other men, he had seen her hanging around the wounded man. "The padre will be having another visitor," he said. "Not a patient this time."

"Ah," Joan said. "Yes. Gumbo's there. And her—so soon. Why, it hasn't been ten minutes since you rode in with him!" She laughed scornfully. "I shouldn't be suspicious, should I?" she said. "Like they are? I wonder if it is a family trait—or taint?"

"You're not like them," he said. "Listening to them has got your mind to running that way. Mine too," he added, his face suddenly solemn. "Not until *he* came, though," and stood erect and waved a hand at Gail, who was riding past, her eyes eager and roving. "So you told Mona you hadn't married him. Do you want them to know—yet?"

"Dade will tell them soon enough," she said and watched him again with that strange look of interest. She added, "When he finds he isn't welcome here."

"He knows that now," he said. "He'll not forget his reception." Something is on her mind, he thought. Not Dade. He saw Mona on the veranda. She was standing alone, as Kathleen and Dade seemed to be talking to each other. "Mona's a maverick there," he said. "She doesn't wear their brand. She'll not tell them anything."

"You like Mona," she said.

"Sure," he said, meaning it.

"She is beautiful," she said and watched his eyes.

"Yes." What is she getting at? he thought. Was she jealous of Mona?

Her eyes were clouded, though wide open as they searched his face. She was biting her lips and trying to smile, but one corner of her mouth drooped dolorously. "She *is* beautiful," she said; "very beautiful. And I—I love her. I love her in spite of her—her *spavin!*"

Startled, he stared at her—and remembered the rock pocket at Bear Flat. "Oh, that!" he said and tried to keep the ecstasy of elation out of his voice. "She told you that?" he said. "That was nothing. You see—"

"I am almost certain I see," she said, holding herself very erect as she walked away from him toward the ranch house.

XIX

Gregg was laughingly deriding Kelso's awkward attempts to ensnare the snubbing post in the corral, but the fighter had better success when, Gregg running away from him, he snapped the loop at him instead of the post, and the boy found himself enmeshed in the coils. With the loop around his shoulders he backed away from the man, tugging to free himself. His cheeks flushed with effort, his eyes shining, he fought to resist Kelso's pull on the rope but was drawn slowly toward the fighter whose battered face was creased in genial wrinkles. "Gotcha, kid!" Kelso shouted as, attracted by the lure of the picture presented there by man and boy, Joan climbed to the beam of a rusted plow and stood on tiptoe to peer over the top of the fence.

"He's a fraud, Mother!" Gregg laughed, his breath coming in gasps. "He says he's muscle bound and can't throw a rope!" Gregg stiffened his body and braced himself against the pull of the rope but he came on, his boot heels cutting deep furrows in the dust of the corral floor, as the fighter, his muscles rippling, slowly but gently pulled him in. Then Gregg, surrendering, threw the rope off and began to box with the fighter, and when the dust began to erupt Joan got down, laughing. Paul, who had been standing there, too, faced her.

He said, "It's exciting here, eh?" and smiled with dry irony. "By George, I don't see how you can stand it! Some people thrive on this sort of thing, though. You particularly. You look great!"

"Thank you, Paul," she said, suspecting him of insincerity. "But it must be tiresome here for you. I don't see how we can make things more exciting, though. It has always been this way—except for the Indians."

"Only more so," he said. "Years ago there'd be trips to town once in a while. And we liked riding then. Now—nothing. No jack. We can't just go to town to gape at things. Say, why don't you take Kathie up— take us up, I mean—on that trip East?" She shook her head and began to walk away from him toward the house, and he followed her, eager.

"I shouldn't care for such things, I'm sure," she said. He was at her side now. "Well, maybe you wouldn't at that," he said. "But you've got us to think of, you know. A little anyway. How about a loan, Joan? God knows we need some jack. We're dead broke. None of us has a sou."

She stopped and faced him. "Yes, I know that," she said. "And I'm sorry things have turned out like this for you—for all of you. I'll do something for you, of course. But there is no place out here where you can spend money, even if you have it. And no place to go to show off what you might buy. It's true, isn't it, that you and the girls didn't come home because you loved home—and me?"

"I've always liked you, Joan," he said. "You know that. Brothers are, of course—well, only brothers. And maybe I did pass you up a bit. Yes, I'll admit that. But that was because I was interested in having a good time. And you were nothing but a kid then."

"What would you do if I gave you some money?" she said.

"I'd go back East and get into some kind of business," he said.

"Gambling, I suppose?"

"Not on your life! I'm through with that stuff. Say, you're a sport after all!" He patted her shoulder. "How much of your roll can you spare?" he said.

She said, "How much would you need to establish yourself in business?"

"Not much," he said. "Fifty thousand would see me through."

She thought a moment and said, "That's quite a price

180

for the kind of affection and respect you have given me, isn't it?" and asked herself how much of that amount she would be willing to pay him out of pity and sympathy. Very little. But she would pay a great deal more than he had asked if doing so would keep the contemptuous derision out of the eyes of the family should they discover there had been no marriage.

"Affection has no price, has it, Sis?" he said.

"Hasn't it?" she said. "Fifty thousand isn't exactly pin money, is it?"

"You've got a million or so," he said. "You wouldn't miss fifty thousand."

She walked on again, sickened by his greed and hypocrisy, yet trying to preserve some shreds of her loyalty to him as a member of the family. He stayed close to her, intent upon persuading her, until suddenly they were near the edge of the veranda where Dade was talking with Kathleen, who was sitting in a chair beside him, and Mona, who was comfortably—though somewhat defiantly—perched in another chair at the farther end.

At Joan's side Paul whispered, "I'll see you later about that loan," and she nodded to him, smiled faintly at Kathleen and brightly at Mona and looked past Dade, who watched her with level gaze and turned his head to look at her as she started to walk across the veranda.

"That prize fighter is bad company for your boy, Joan," said Kathleen. "I've just been talking with your husband about it, and he has promised to speak to

181

Gregg." She looked at Mona. "And to Mr. Kelso," she added.

"Bat will love that," said Mona, winking at Joan.

"Gregg is quite capable of choosing his own friends," said Joan.

All of her guests were out of the house, somewhere, and Joan, changing her dress in her room toward the end of the afternoon, was listening to sounds to which she had become accustomed—to the neighing of horses and the bawling of calves in the corrals; the lowing of milch cows in the pasture; the ringing of the blacksmith's hammer on the anvil; the voices of Mexican gardeners; a dog barking, and the shrill cries of children playing. Through the breeze-blown curtains of the windows she could see Gregg and Kelso sitting on a bench in front of the stable, and Gumbo and Gail riding toward the wooded country beyond Antelope Creek where the canyon began. In the padre's garden was the padre, his gray-clad figure erect, watching the riders, and Joan wondered what his thoughts were, seeing them together so much. For Gumbo's second convalescence was longer than the first, and he had reported to her that his wound was "showing stubborn." The padre had explained it another way, saying, "She's attractive, but the boy will get over it," and had kept his face straight, though his eyes had twinkled. Webster would have understood and sent him to rejoin his outfit, but Webster had gone to the North Branch and had been away for a week, riding there with Joe Lathrop, who had finished his season's buying and was staying on at the ranch for a while. And Joan wanted no scenes with Gail.

Avoiding Dade as much as possible, seeing him only at mealtimes or when she could not otherwise evade him, she knew he would bring about a meeting with her sooner or later, for she had perceived that by continually watching her movements he was seeking such an opportunity. But she had not expected the meeting to occur when it did, with all the others away and herself and Dade in the hall, almost at the door of her room—which she was occupying with Mona. She instantly suspected he knew the others were not in the house and that he had deliberately contrived to be in the hall at this minute, for he was standing there as she stepped out of her room, and was so close to her that she could not re-enter the room except by pushing past him. With the sensation of being trapped she faced him indignantly and saw the arrogance of his past conquest of her in his bold and confident look.

"Well," he said. "Here we are—at last—alone," and moved nearer. "My wife now," he whispered and tried to put an arm around her.

She evaded him by stepping back. She was not thinking of herself but of him, of how designing and how entirely treacherous he was. She was curiously intent, trying to remember what he had looked like in those other days. He had been fine somehow. Now he was dissipated and coarse. She thought he had been clean and vital. Now he was gross and, as Kathleen had said, "shopworn." He had been persuasive, and now he was arrogant and insinuatingly suggestive of his former power over her. Her own calmness amazed her, though her throat and lips were tight with hate and disgust.

"That's over, Frank," she said and almost smiled over the way his eyes changed expression—how they lost their arrogance and boldness and grew suddenly astonished.

"Over?" he said. "How—over? What do you mean? You sent the foreman to meet me, didn't you? You wanted to see me but you've been giving me the runaround."

"That's what you thought," she said, "when Webster went to Hackett's camp." She was pleased to find she could look at him with calm disinterestedness, with indifference to what he had been to her. It was as if nothing had ever happened between them.

"Listen, kid," he said. "What's coming off here? Is this a phony deal?"

"It's as bogus as you are, Frank," she said and saw his face grow longer.

"Hell," he said; "I'm your husband."

"That's what you think. That's what the family thinks," she said and watched his lips go into a pout of disappointment.

"Look here," he said, squinting his eyes at her, speculatively watching her. "Somebody's got their signals crossed. Your foreman told me there was a marked card or two in this deck. That we are supposed to be married because your family is here and you have to produce a father for Gregg. He told me I was *it*. That we'd been married by a wandering parson and that there was a record of the marriage in the family Bible. Now you say I'm *not* married to you. There's something screwy here!"

"You mean, of course, that things don't suit you," she said and interpreted his stare as bewilderment. "That you can't have things the way you want them. You can't, of course. Things have changed since you went away. I have changed. At least I think I have. So much that I now detest you. And the longer you stay here—"

"I see," he said. "I'm in the wrong pew. And in church. You want me to get out." His eyes were narrowed, derisive, searching. "That's what you want most right now," he added. "When I came here your foreman told me I was to play up to the husband role. Now the scene changes and I'm to be thrown out on my ear. The errant lover assumes the responsibilities of fatherhood to help the noble though wayward gal who finds it convenient to fool her family, and becomes a sacrificing husband and a bum."

"Very affecting," she said and was able to give him a little twisted smile of contempt, while she wondered about the shoddy quality of his manhood and found it harder than ever to understand why she had once been so foolish about him. She added, "Did you ever do anything unselfishly, Frank?"

"What's the stall now?" he said and watched her suspiciously. "I'll bite. I didn't. Why should I?"

"No—of course. That would be foolish, wouldn't it?"

185

she said and laughed at herself for asking the question. Was it because she still had a faint hope that he hadn't lost all the qualities that she had once been innocent enough to idealize? Well, he would be mercenary, of course, like the family, and she wondered if she should pay the price he would ask—that all of them would ask—and thank God that she could then be rid of them, never to see them again, and to attempt to shut them out of her memory. She laughed again as she recalled the anxiety and yearning that had tortured her for eleven years—the waiting and longing for him and her family; the hopes she had built; the dreams she had dreamed; the plans she had made. She thought of Paul, of the look in his eyes, of his fawning insincerity when he had said: "Affection has no price—has it, Sis?"

She said, trying to keep the bitterness out of her voice, trying to be calm, "What *did* you come here for, Frank?"

He was quick to catch the change in her voice and stepped toward her again. "That's a funny question to ask," he said. "I came here for you, of course. Let's be sensible about this. We'll say I made a mistake in leaving you as I did. I admit it. But I was pretty young, and so were you; and maybe neither of us realized what we were doing. We were just kids, falling in love and getting scared of what was going to happen. I can see that now. I've been seeing it for quite a while. I didn't write to you until I got to Tucson because I never knew what to say to you and I didn't know how sore you were."

She kept backing away, staying out of reach of his arms, for she felt that if he touched her she would scream with horror, and, hearing her, Kelso would come running to her from the stable. She was shaking her head, not being able to understand how he could pretend, how he could even think she could believe him, or that his explanation was plausible.

"Yes," she said. "As you say—it is funny. Why you came, I mean. Very funny. You are funny—in a way. Most people are. Funny to other people whom they don't understand. But perhaps that isn't just what you mean. I think you mean I am being absurd in asking why you came here. Absurd for wondering, when I should know without asking. If you come any closer I shall call for Mr. Kelso, who is sitting in front of the stable with Gregg!"

He stopped following her and stared at her, his senses at last confirming what his continuing study of her had revealed to him—that she was fine and great, and true to herself. He was amazed, yet cynical, and enraged and disgusted with himself for having deserted this magnificent woman. He said, "It looks like you've grown out of my class," and knew he must drop the pretense of having come back to win her again. "All right," he said. "I didn't expect you to fall for me again. I came back to see if I could grab some of the jack you've made."

"I have been curious," she said. "Did you hear of my money before you reached Tucson, or did Gumbo tell you about it?"

"Gumbo!" he said. "Do you mean that wild gazabo

187

who busted my casekeeper's hand in Delafan's place?" His shoulders jerked nervously. "Is he the fellow who has been riding around with Gail?"

"Yes."

"Holy smoke!" he said. "That man is sudden death!"

"He doesn't like you," she said. "And he remembers you from the time you were here before. But he won't bother my husband—or the man he thinks is my husband. Is that clear to you?"

"Plenty," he said.

"All right, Frank. Now tell me where you heard about my having some money."

"The newspapers in the East were full of it awhile ago," he said. "They carried descriptions of the ranch and you. 'Cattle Queen' they called you. Your family gave them the tip."

"So that's where they got the idea," she said.

"What idea?" he said, watching her.

She ignored the question and asked, "Did the newspapers say the family intended to come out here and take me back East with them?"

"That's what the reporters wrote," he said. "One of them got fanciful. He said, in big headlines, 'Cattle Queen to visit East. Someday some man will be her king. She's single. Have your proposals ready.'" He thought, regret stirring him, "Her king! I could have been that to her. Now I'm a tramp." He said, "Are you thinking of going East?"

She started. "Was I thinking?" she said. "No—only laughing. At people. At all of us. Of how things do not turn out the way we expect them to. At how we make plans—to see them wrecked." She looked steadily at him and spoke steadily, "Money is very important to most people. How much do you expect to get—from me?"

"I've got to do some thinking about that," he said, his eyes gleaming slyly. "There's a new angle—the newspapers. There'd be a new sensation for them to print. How about this for a headline: 'Frank Dade, gambler, is father of Cattle Queen's child. Allege old romance sans marriage'?" He said, his smile mocking, "Thank you for mentioning the newspapers."

She was frightened and said huskily, "But they couldn't say that! The marriage record is in the Bible!"

"Sure," he said. "The record was there—is there. In your foreman's handwriting. Kathleen compared it with his writing on some papers in his office. That's all there is. Of course you could go to court about it. But would you want to go to court? I'd make it my business to be there, to testify that the marriage hadn't been legal— that there had been only the romance. But for about a hundred thousand I would keep my mouth shut tighter than a clam's. That would be an easy way to get rid of a guy who might have been a king."

She thought a moment, looking at him. Then she said, smiling at him, "I'll think it over, Frank. Perhaps it has been worth that much—having you here to look at, and to realize that things might have been worse if I had really married you."

XX

That night as dusk drifted in, spreading thin on the plains and deepening to blackness around the bases of the hills, Webster and Lathrop rode in.

Passing the ranch house, Webster had seen lights in the kitchen and one other room only. It was so dark by then that he would not have known anyone was on the veranda if he had not heard voices there. He did not hear Joan's voice. He and the buyer slid from their saddles at the stable door, stood for a moment in the light of a lantern inside the doorway there, and then walked to the foreman's shack, where they lit an oil lamp, washed themselves in water from the trough under the windmill, brushed the dust from their boots and trousers, changed shirts and went to the mess house for supper. In the light from the lamp on the long table between them Lathrop studied the foreman's face and saw a frown of concentration there.

"It's the first time I ever saw Hackett stirred up like that," said the buyer. "He says he's been hearing it for days."

"The boys are talking about it," said Webster. He stared into the darkness beyond the doorway. "And there's no way to shut their mouths or to keep them from thinking about what they've heard," he said. He did not eat but sat there staring at his empty plate. "Tom Hackett was double tongued about it—as he always is," he added. "Wanted to know why I hadn't split with him—if it was true that I'd been taking her money. He doesn't *want* to think I would cheat her."

"He was raving mad because it had got around," said Lathrop. "Coming from nowhere like that and nobody responsible."

"He didn't ask me to deny it," said Webster. "He just said, 'Damn their hides—whoever they are—for even thinking a thing like that!' You weren't there then to see the way he looked at me."

"It was odd seeing the way the boys watched you," said Lathrop. "You didn't see them looking, because when you looked at them they were looking at something else. They didn't like to think you would do a thing like that. They don't believe it but they wish you'd show them that you didn't take her money that way. What are you going to do about it?"

"Nothing now," said Webster. He got up and walked to the door, hearing hoofbeats outside, and peered into the darkness. He came back to the table, dropped into the chair he had vacated and began to put food on his plate. "Gumbo," he said to the buyer. "And Gail. Just in from a ride. She's gone to the house. He'll be in here for grub. I've been hearing reports about their rides together. From the padre. There's more than a bullet wound bothering him."

"It's her," said Lathrop. "She's slick."

"I'll find out," said Webster. "He's a good steady boy. He remembers Dade when Dade was here before. But he didn't want to let on." He ate a few bites, with pauses between to listen. "He couldn't know about what we've been doing," he said.

"Joan will find out," said Lathrop. "She's sure to. It will get to her. What then?"

"She won't believe it—at first," Webster said and listened again. "There'll have to be conclusive evidence—the kind that she'll have to be sure of. She's always trusted me. That's why we have been able to do the things we have done."

"You're such a son of a gun," said Lathrop. At a thought his jaw dropped. "She'll quit selling to me," he said.

"I'll take the blame," said Webster and added, "Here's Gumbo now."

Gumbo came in. He stopped just inside the door and looked innocently at them, but the flush on his face betrayed him and he nervously rubbed his chin. "Hello," he said. "I was scared supper was over."

The cook had heard him come in and now peered at him from the kitchen door. He grumbled, "Late again. You're getting to be a regular night owl," and disappeared.

Webster said, "Married men don't have that trouble with cooks. There'd be no reason for it. Married men are always home for supper." He kicked a chair close to him and watched Gumbo drop into it. The chair was at Webster's left where he could see Gumbo's face in the lamplight. He waited until the cook, still grumbling, brought Gumbo's food in. Then they all ate, in silence, Webster seemingly paying no attention to the rider.

He said, at last, "How's your side coming along?"

"Passable," said Gumbo. He ate fast, gulping his food as if in a hurry to finish.

"You been riding?" said Webster.

"She's been wanting to see the country," said Gumbo.

"Strange to her, I expect?"

"Not exactly. She wanted to see it again," said Gumbo. He laughed nervously. "I thought of that too—her wanting to see what she already knows about."

"She knows more than you think," said Webster. "Does she tell you what she knows? Or does she pretend she knows nothing so that you can air your knowledge? Some women have that way of leading a man on—making him think he's wise."

Gumbo laughed. "You're laying it on strong," he said. "I was wise to her right away. Pumping me. Mostly about Dade. But my forgettery is better than my memory. She seemed to be interested in a drifting parson. She called him a 'Campbellite.' I didn't have to pretend that I didn't know him or had never heard of him." He started to laugh but looked at Webster and stared in pained astonishment. "Hell," he said; "that's what she wanted to know, eh? I'm a boxhead!"

"Don't kick yourself too much," said Webster. "She'd know that you've never been familiar with parsons. She would have showed disappointment if you had remembered seeing one around here."

"That's a fact!" said Gumbo. "She seemed tickled that I hadn't seen any parson—besides the padre."

"She say anything about Lathrop here?"

"Not much. Only wanted to know how much he had

been paying Joan for beef stock for the last few years. She's got a friend who works for the Chicago livestock market."

"You told her?"

"What I'd heard. Thirty, average. Some years more, some years less."

"She say anything about that?"

Gumbo blushed and stared at his plate. "Said it was funny that Joan's records showed only about twenty, average," he said. "I told her the record must be cock-eyed," he added and got up, leaving most of the food on his plate. He went out, pulling his hat down over his forehead, saying a faint, "So long."

Webster shoved his plate back and looked at the buyer. "Gumbo not remembering the Campbellite parson bothers me most," he said. He got up. "I'm going to stretch my legs," he said. "Alone, if you don't mind," and went out.

That same night Joan was in bed, lying on her right side, wide awake. Through the south window she could see the moon rising, low over the mountaintops, sailing through the fleecy cloud waves of an indigo-blue sky with a star-spangled setting. Mona was curled up close to her, one hand resting on her shoulder. They had been—and were—talking about Dade.

"The chump!" said Mona. "Thinking you'd fall for him again! So he said the reason he didn't write was that he wouldn't have known what to say to you? But when he got here he wasn't tongue-tied. And you gave him the gate! Smart kid!" She patted Joan's shoulder. "Webster's worth a million of him!"

Webster! Joan stirred restlessly, and Mona sighed sleepily.

Everything was now clear to Joan—clear and serene, like the sky up there. There were tricks and snares in this lovely mystery of life, but once you knew what you wanted the mystery was solved. It was because people did not know what they wanted that they got entangled. If she had taken Webster when her chance had come she wouldn't have missed eleven years of happiness. She now knew she had wanted him, and still wanted him. But could she have him? Was that jealousy—that sudden disturbing apprehension which had stabbed at her only today when she had talked with Webster in front of his shack? She had felt nothing like that in her relations with Dade—not while he had been with her, or during the years he had been away, when she did not know what he had been doing. The country had come out of darkness and she saw it stretching away, faintly luminous in the moonlight, lovely and calm—so calm and quiet and beautiful that it drew her thoughts out there and sent them wandering to days when she and Webster had roamed this country until she knew it so completely that she could walk through it blindfolded. She had solved the mystery of the sepulchral silence. Silence was old, for it had been here when the world began, and man's activities had not disturbed it. She had interpreted the message of the encompassing desolation as serenity and peace. The monotony of life in this land had never affected her, for to her there had never been, and was not, monotony. There was unchanging and steadfast rugged life. The land stayed as it was—as it had been, and as it would always be— the soft sand stretches, the gravel, the clay, the rocks, the mountains, the creek. She knew when the paloverde bark was greenest; when the Spanish dagger blossoms came; when the pinyon tree put forth its edible nuts; when the scrub oak freshened in the spring, and when the color of the sagebrush turned from gray-green to purple. She knew at what season of the year the barrel cactus, the saguaro, bore its pale yellow flowers, and when the mesquite trees in the lowlands became most filmy. Monotony was not in nature; it was in one's thoughts. The monotony of satiation, which made one yearn for a change. Nature did not change. Only people were changeable. Nature had its ways, its moods. It was beautiful or ugly, or pleasant or cruel, in season. You could anticipate nature's moods but not the moods of people. New foliage would come in the spring—every spring. Grass would come for the herds. Water would be somewhere obtainable. The earth would yield its crops for man and beast. The rains would come—or be stored. The sun would shine; the moon would shift the tides—or romance, and man would die. This was what she loved—the certainty of nature and of the land. Its honesty; the cosmic scope of its purpose; the invariability of its productivity; its unswerving purpose to serve. Why couldn't people be like that? Why should they be like the family and Dade? But only Webster was important to her now—Webster and the enthralling beauty of this night. When she saw a grove of cotton-woods being drenched in the liquid silver streaming down upon them, their drooping fronds dripping mellow, satiny light and the hard ground beneath shimmering in mottled pattern of glowing white in shadowy tracery, she slipped softly out of bed and went to the window.

Webster saw a light in his shack and a moving shadow inside so he knew Lathrop was there waiting for him. He was not yet ready to go in so he climbed to the top of the corral fence, rolled and lit a cigarette and sat there thinking. Gumbo too. It hit him pretty hard to remember how Gumbo had looked—embarrassed and avoiding his eyes. The poison being spread by the family was hard for the men to take. They were squirming and reluctant, but their way of avoiding him showed him the poison was working.

There were no lights in the house now so he could be about the business he had in mind. Gumbo had mentioned Joan's records which were in a set of books which she kept on a shelf in his office. He had never looked in them, and only intended to glance at them now, to satisfy himself about Gumbo's remark about them, to see if the family had got their information there. His own records were on shelves on the wall above his own desk and in pigeonholes in the desk itself. He was no bookkeeper and had an aversion to dry details, so the information the family might find in his own records would be confusing to them, as they had many times been to him. He slid down from the corral fence and walked toward the house, using no particular stealth, for he often worked in the office while Joan and the help were asleep, and they had got accustomed to that. No doors were ever closed except in stormy weather, so the only noise he made in mounting to the veranda, crossing it and entering his office was the faintly jingling sound of his spurs. The low moon, striking the veranda aslant from the southeast, showed him the well-worn stone floor and the vacant chairs standing there, the wide-open door to the living room and an awry rectangle of moon-light on the floor inside the room. He lit the oil lamp on his desk, adjusted the wick so that the flame would not smudge the chimney, slid into his chair and leaned back to continue his thinking. The flickering light beams from the oil lamp penetrated into the living room through the inside office door, tinging with yellow tones the edge of a buffalo robe lying there on the floor. Smoke from the cigarette between his lips floated lazily to the outside door and was turned into silvery writhing wisps by the moonlight.

The records he sought had been disturbed. While he had been away to the North Branch with Lathrop his desk had been rifled, and the records restored in hap-hazard fashion. For more than an hour he worked with them, straightening them out, his rage growing. The family had been through everything. For years he had anticipated their visit, and Dade's, but he had not expected this. They were all asleep now, having found what they wanted. Was Joan asleep too? He fell to wondering about her—how she was making it with Dade; if the family continued their venomous persecution; how Gregg was getting on with his new-found father; if Mona was as sarcastic as ever, and what Kelso secretly thought of the family and Dade. But he kept thinking of Joan's manner the day he had met her in front of his shack; of her thinly concealed emotion when she had talked of Mona's beauty and her "spavin"; of her inconsistency in being jealous of his trivial incident with Mona when she resented his jealousy of Dade. But he could understand the torture she had been through, and how she had waited for Dade to come back to her— waited alone and patiently, trusting in Dade's manliness and being neglected and ignored by her family. While he had been nursing his jealousy of Dade, and his hate, what had her thoughts been? What were they now, with Dade in the house, she hating him, and the family greed hedging her in? There was a rustling sound in the living room, a soft footfall, and he saw her come into the radius of the lamp glow at the inside door which she had seen while she had still been in the hall, just after closing the door of her room, having been lured by the beauty of the night. She was startled, seeing him there, and pleased, too, for though her hands went up to her throat, her voice had a leap in it as she whispered, "Bob, it's you!"

"It's me," he said and saw the pulse in her throat throbbing as if from excitement. He could understand that excitement. She here with him, and Dade and the family in the house, not too many feet distant. Her face was white, too, whiter than usual, and her eyes had a strained expression, as if she had been thinking too much, or had been staring too long at something. She wore, he was certain, nothing much—something light under a soft-looking dressing gown which covered her to her slippered toes. The garment had a fluffy collar that snuggled her shoulders negligently, and her hair on the right side was disordered as if she had been lying on it.

"I couldn't sleep," she said, and he knew that thoughts of Dade and the family had been bothering her. "I didn't know you had got back," she added. "I thought you were still at North Branch."

All alone again, he thought. More alone than ever, even with them around! An instinct to protect her, always strong in him, was straining at his heart now. "I had some work to do here," he said and was astonished to hear how husky his voice sounded to him.

It sounded strange to her, too, for she peered curiously at him, wondering what had happened to him. "What work?" she said. "Was everything all right on the North Branch? How did the herd look to Mr. Lathrop?"

"Fair," he said, answering her last questions first. "The tally," he added. He got up and faced her, and was so close to her that he could have touched her, and almost did, his longing for her making him tremble inside. "Under two thousand head," he said. "Not as good as last year. And the price has dropped. The

200

Eastern market is slow and there is little construction work going on west of the Mississippi." He didn't want to talk about the cattle but could think of nothing else to say. There was something hesitant, something wistful about her, in the way she stood there, in the way her mouth looked—sad, as if she was about to cry. She was wondering what she would do—how she would feel, if she discovered that he loved Mona.

"Price," she said, frowning. "Money. Must everything be tied up with money? That's all I hear. Paul wants fifty thousand—as a loan. Dade wants a hundred thousand. I don't know what Kathleen and Gail will want. Oh, I am so sick of it all."

What her family wanted wasn't important to him. She could give them anything she wanted to give them. That was her business. But Dade was different. "A hundred thousand!" he said. "What for?"

She watched his eyes and saw the rage in them. She knew a wrong word would spur him to take a vengeance long meditated. "He knows now that his visit here is—was—wasted," she said, stumbling over her words but wanting him to understand. "He knows now that he isn't wanted." Her voice had lowered to a tight whisper, but it was steady and earnest, for tonight her vision was clear and she could see far back into the past. "He never loved me," she said. "The family never loved me. All any of them want is money. I wish I had never made it. I wish you hadn't been here to help me make it—to make it for me. For you don't—don't—either."

"Don't—what?" he said, trembling. He was scared now, more than he had ever been scared, for he saw that happiness was nearer to him than it had ever been. "Don't love you?" he said, his voice shaking and rasping deep in his throat. "You poor kid!" he said.

She was in his arms now, shaking and quivering, but light and soft as she looked up at him, her eyes searching his, hoping, doubt leaving them when she saw the light in his and felt his arms tighten around her, drawing her close with a fierce gentleness. The touch of her cold cheek against his made his heart swell with wild ecstasy. There was something here of which he had dreamed—her cool arms around his neck, their softness as they clung to him; the smooth touch of her hands on his face as she held him and looked up at him; the deep-glowing sweetness in her eyes as he kissed her and looked down at her. Better than his dreams. This was real. To make sure he was not dreaming he held her tight and looked out into the moonlit world in which, a short time ago, there had been only darkness and his own troubled thoughts. Then she had seemed to be miles away. Now she was in his arms and clinging tightly to him. Never had rapture like this held him; never had his thoughts of the future been so enchanting.

XXI

In the gray morning light it was no different for either of them. Sitting on the edge of his bed in his shack, Webster looked out at the willows along the creek and nodded at them. "You are not as graceful as she is," he said and saw Lathrop lying on his back, wide awake, looking at him.

"Crazy as a loon," said the buyer. "There's nobody around here but me, and nobody could call me graceful. Or maybe you was thinking of Gail—of how she hooked Gumbo. Have you figured out what you are going to do?" He watched Webster's face. "You were worried last night," he said.

"Old age has driven the romance out of you," said Webster. "Can you remember when you proposed to your wife?"

Lathrop scratched his head and looked surprised. "By George, you've got me!" he said and studied the foreman's face, seeing the light in his eyes and the high color showing through the bronzed skin of his face. "It's been a long time ago," he added. "A man forgets such things. But I can remember that at the time I was as tickled as you are." He swung around and sat on the edge of the bed, facing Webster. "I saw a light in the foreman's office last night," he said. "You didn't get to bed until just before daylight. By George! The boss!"

"We'll be married as soon as the family goes—and Dade," said Webster. "The padre will perform the ceremony. There will be a license, this time. It will be as tight as the law can make it."

"You don't say!" said Lathrop. Some of Joan's story had been told him by Webster. The rest he had guessed. "Well, that's fine!" he said. "That's what should have happened years ago! So it don't make much difference

203

about the Campbellite parson?" He squinted his eyes at Webster. "Are you sure you deserve her?" he said. "She's a mighty fine woman. That's what my wife said about her—and nobody's fooling *her!*"

"I'll be wanting her near me until I get older than you," said Webster. "And I'll never play poker if it bothers her." He got up and took off his night robe. "And I'll not be forgetting when I proposed to her," he added.

Lying on her right side, Joan had watched the moonlight become more and more pale until at last it faded into a gray dawn in which the fronds on the trees in the cottonwood grove looked green again and the grass in the pasture showed a delicate blue sheen. "It seems natural to be here," she said, thinking of last night when she had been in Webster's arms. "It is where I always wanted to be," and saw Mona, propped on an arm, looking at her.

"Where is *here?*" said Mona. "And *where is* where you always wanted to be?"

"*Here* is where Bob is," said Joan. "And *where* is there too. Mona, we are engaged!"

"For Gawd's sake!" said Mona. "It happened! And right under my nose! Where? How?"

"In his office," said Joan breathlessly. "I couldn't sleep. You know we were talking about Dade, and you began to snore. So I started to go out on the veranda. But I didn't get there—until later. There was a light in his office, and he was there working. I didn't know it was going to happen. But, Mona, I have always loved

204

him. I knew it last night when—when—"

"When you found out where *there* is," said Mona. "And I never snore!" she added.

Joan said, "You don't mind, Mona?"

"Mind what?" said Mona. "Mind that you got him? Why, I've been pulling for you, haven't I? And knocking that chump, Dade! Webster was made for you, kid. From the beginning. You got sidetracked by that mug, Dade, but that don't mean you've got to spend the rest of your life weeping and moaning. Take him, my child, and thank God you've got him. He's the best sample of a man I've seen in a long time!"

Gregg was awakened by his mother kissing him. Her face was radiant and her eyes shone with a light he had never seen in them. She hugged him tightly as she knelt at his bedside, and then held his face in her hands and patted his cheeks, and smoothed his tousled hair and kissed his forehead.

"Gee, you look happy, Mother!" he said. "Has anything happened? Is it good news of some kind?"

She hugged him again and laughed. He thought there was a look of solemnity about her and he stared at her, puzzled. He had never seen her like this. "I know," he said. "You are riding and you like to ride. Who with?"

"With Bob Webster," she said and stood erect and smiled at him.

"That's the suit you bought last year," he said. "I like it, but you've never worn it. It looks great! Where are you going?"

"Just riding," she said. "Not far. To some places I have almost forgotten." She went to a window and looked out, then to the door and looked back at him. "Don't get up right away," she said. "You can't go anywhere with Mr. Kelso today. Today is the day for your lessons, and the padre will be expecting you." From where she stood the smooth satiny skin of Gregg's cheeks lured her, and she went to him and kissed him again—his cheeks and lips, their baby softness still lingering there in spite of his growing-up stature. Then she went out of the room into the hall, and down the hall to the living room, which was empty, with the door of the foreman's office open, as it had been when she had seen Webster in it last night; and out upon the veranda, to see that Dade and the family were already there, and that Webster was riding toward them from the stable, leading a horse for her to ride.

Dade was walking back and forth on the ground in front of the veranda, and she looked past him as she always did. But she smiled and said "Good morning" to Gail and Kathleen and Paul, and tried to solve the mystery of their expressionless faces—though she thought Paul looked anxious, probably about the fifty-thousand-dollar loan. Mona was still in her room, and Joan could see Kelso sitting in front of the foreman's shack with Lathrop. Concertedly they watched Webster ride toward the veranda with the led horse.

"It's early for riding, isn't it, Joan?" said Kathleen.

"That depends upon why you are riding," Joan said.

"And with whom," said Gail.

"This is business, I suppose?" said Kathleen.

"Certainly."

"Oh, of course—business," said Kathleen.

"With Spotted Elk," said Joan. She saw Dade's face turn pale and Paul suddenly sit erect. Paul said, "You'll have somebody with you besides Webster?"

"The Maricopas are friendly," said Joan. "I've seen to that. But just to be on the safe side Tom Hackett and some of the Bear Flat outfit will ride with us to Spotted Elk's camp."

"Friends!" said Dade. "How about the six Maricopas Gumbo and his men killed?"

"That's what our business is about," said Joan. Smiling and calm, she waited for Webster and met him at the edge of the veranda where she mounted and rode away with him. They went past the stable, past the foreman's shack, where Kelso and the buyer waved at them, then rode into the wild country beyond.

The family and Dade watched them until they vanished behind a ridge in the direction of the padre's hacienda. Paul rubbed his chin. "They won't pick up the Bear Flat outfit going that way," he said. "Bear Flat is the other way."

"Sure," agreed Dade.

Gail laughed and enjoyed their perplexity. "Maybe it's a lovers' ride," she said, looking at the gambler. "Or maybe they're going to look for that Campbellite parson." She smiled at all of them. "There wasn't any Campbellite parson," she said. "Nor any other parson." She looked with level eyes at Dade. "Was

207

there?" she asked.

"Sure," said Dade, remembering Gumbo and his promise to Webster on the ride to the ranch house from Hackett's camp.

"Gumbo says there wasn't a parson of any kind," said Gail. "That there has never been a parson around here. Not at that time, or since."

"Was Gumbo around here then?" said Dade.

"He was," said Gail. "And he remembers you. But he can't remember that you ever married Joan. And he says it's strange that if you did marry her, she didn't insist on the padre performing the ceremony. He was her teacher for a good many years, and she loves him. Why should she permit a strange parson to marry her? We've thought of that, too, haven't we, Kathie?"

Kathleen said, "What did the Campbellite parson look like, Mr. Dade? And who were the witnesses to the marriage?" Her look probed the gambler's eyes and found them wary but doubting. He suspected what this talk portended, but there had been no witness and no marriage, and he did not know how much the sisters knew.

"I don't remember," he said. "That was a long time ago, you know, and I haven't got much of a memory for faces." His look became amused insolence.

"That's true, I think," said Kathleen. "It took you eleven years to remember Joan."

"Look here," said Dade. "Don't get fresh. You forgot her yourself until you discovered she had scads of kale!" He grinned maliciously at them. "Then you

208

rushed to the newspapers and told them she was your sister."

"So that's where you found out about her having money!" said Kathleen. "We had been wondering."

Paul stirred and cleared his throat. "I've been doing a bit of wondering too," he said.

"About what, Paul?" said Gail.

"About this marriage stuff," Paul said and watched Dade's face. "About the way Joan treated you when you came here, and how she has dispensed a husband's privileges since." He laughed.

They all saw the sudden cold fury in the gambler's eyes. "Damned snoopers!" he said.

Kathleen smiled with malice. Paul wondered if he should feel offended. Gail laughed with offensive harshness and said, "One can't help seeing, can one?" She waited until all of them were looking at her. "There is so very much to see," she said then. "Things a husband ought to see. Perhaps to be told about." She hesitated, seeming reluctant to continue. "One doesn't like to tell on one's sister, especially to her sister's husband," she went on, "but a married man has certain rights and we are all morally obligated to see that such rights are not violated." She looked at Kathleen. "Shall I tell Mr. Dade what I saw last night after I came back from a ride with Gumbo?"

Kathleen said, "Why, yes, of course. I think he ought to know, even if Joan is our sister."

"She said Paul wanted fifty thousand dollars from her, as a loan," Gail went on. "That she didn't know how much Kathleen and myself would want from her, and that your price was one hundred thousand, Mr. Dade. Webster was furious. 'A hundred thousand!' he said. 'What for?' And Joan answered him, saying that you now knew you weren't wanted here; that you had never loved her; that none of us had ever loved her, and that all we wanted from her was her money. After that she was in his arms kissing him. And I couldn't hear any more."

"Where was this?" said Dade. He had seen jealousy in Webster in their ride from Hackett's camp to the ranch house on the day he had arrived here, and it had amused him. Now a sudden hate was raging in him.

"Why, I had just got back from a ride with Gumbo," said Gail with what she thought was disarming hesitation. "I was too tired to go to bed and so I just stretched out on the davenport in the living room, intending to go to bed after I had got rested. But I couldn't sleep, and after a while—it must have been toward midnight—I saw Webster in his office looking over some papers." She smiled blandly at Kathleen, who knew what papers Webster had been looking at, and resumed: "Not long after that Joan came through the hall into the living room and stopped at the door of Webster's office. It was all rather affecting, the way they kissed and fondled each other. They seemed to be very much in love. From what I could gather they have been in love with each other all the time, ever since they were kids. They went out on the veranda after that and looked at the moon, and held hands and kissed some more, and told each other fairy tales about how they had felt while Webster had felt she had belonged to Mr. Dade. I think watching them would have made even you jealous, Mr. Dade. Some husbands, watching them, would have lost their heads. It's bad enough even hearing about it. Such things *are* tragic, aren't they?" She was looking at the gambler, but he had turned his pallid face and burning eyes away from her, and so she smiled faintly and winked at Kathleen.

Paul was staring at the floor. "Murder has been done for less than that!" he said. "I've always thought Webster was that kind of a guy. Damn him; if it was my wife he had monkeyed with, I'd kill him!"

"Now he has gone away with her," said Gail. "Probably they made it up between them last night—or this morning. It was nearly daylight when the party broke up." She was enjoying their reaction to her recital. She had told Kathleen and Paul earlier in the morning— telling Kathleen while both of them were still in bed, and both going to Paul's room afterward. For whether or not Joan and the gambler had been, or were, married, they now saw the foreman looming as a formidable and potential wrecker of their plans. They could handle the gambler, but Webster would be obstinate and difficult.

Cynically Gail justified the attitude of the family. They had to protect Joan from the gambler, who had deserted her and returned to her only when he had discovered she had grown wealthy; and from Webster, who couldn't really love her after what had happened to her and was merely after her money and control of the

211

ranch. She was enjoying Dade's agitation as much as she had enjoyed Webster's puzzled rage over his discovery, last night, that the records in his desk had been tampered with. The gambler's cold eyes were blazing with fury, and Gail was pleasantly astonished, though skeptical. He was really jealous, she thought. About the money, of course. The hundred thousand he wanted could not be wheedled or bullied out of Webster. And of course there was his hurt vanity to be considered, for he had been superseded in Joan's affections. It would be too bad, to be sure, if the gambler were to act upon Paul's suggestion about killing Webster. But if it happened there would, fortunately, be no Webster to interfere with the family's managing of Joan.

She said, reflectively laughing, "There goes your fifty thousand, Paul. And Mr. Dade's hundred thousand, I'm afraid. It really seems to be serious with them. And would you say that Joan deliberately rode in the wrong direction with him? Just to let us know that she doesn't care what we think?"

Dade did not speak. He walked back and forth in front of the veranda for a few minutes, then abruptly mounted it and entered the house. Going straight to his room, he drew a chair to a front window, sank into it and stared out into the white sunlight. In the glare he could see the gray shapes of the corral fences; the shacks of the Mexican laborers and the married riders; the huge stable; the other buildings; the horses in the corrals; the calves and some cattle; the great stacks of hay left over from the last winter; the big gardens, and other evidences of the vastness and prosperity of this place. He could feel, and had felt all along, the atmosphere of quiet power and plenty here, and the casual acceptance of this opulence by Joan and her riders. This was an empire over which he might have reigned. He might have been king and millionaire but he had missed. Now, with Webster winning Joan, he would lose the hundred thousand he had named as a price for his silence.

XXII

Sitting there, he saw Tom Hackett riding in, his long legs dangling below the wide saddle skirts, his heels bearing against the edges of the ox-bow stirrups he used. He was riding straight up, loose and jointless as his pony racked along with effortless ease. He had come out of the eastern glare like an apparition, and when, in passing the veranda and seeing the family there, he waved a hand at them, Dade saw the heavy gun he wore lying against his leg, and remembered how, when he had been in the hoodlum wagon at Bear Flat, with Webster there waiting to escort him to the ranch house, Hackett had urged him to shoot the foreman. He now realized that he should have acted upon Hackett's suggestion. If he had killed Webster then, he would be ruler here now. He watched Hackett ride past the house, not stopping at the veranda, for he had no business with the family and liked none of them.

Dade got up, kicked the chair in which he had been

sitting, overturning it and malevolently watching it as it crashed into a wall. Damn it! he thought, my life has been full of missed opportunities! No more of them would be missed. He opened the door of his room and walked down the hall to its extreme end, where a south window overlooked the stable, a wide section of the corrals, the bunk and mess houses, the gardens, the foreman's shack and the stretch of wild country into which Webster and Joan had vanished awhile ago. Along the edge of the canyon beyond Antelope Creek he saw two horses and their riders moving, and he recognized the riders as Webster and Joan. In front of the foreman's shack were Lathrop and Kelso, just sitting there. He saw Hackett ride to the stable door where a stableman took charge of his pony and led it to the watering trough, Hackett turning away and knocking his hat against his boots to get the dust out of it, and then using it to slap the dust out of his trousers. He put the hat back on his head and drew the brim well down, and walked toward the buyer and the prize fighter, slapping his shirt with his hands, dust puffs rising at each slap.

Dade heard their laughter, faint but unmistakably genial, and thought of how a few days ago, with things looking well for him, he had felt rather good and in a mood to laugh. This morning was not like other mornings, to him. There was tension here now, and hostility, to be felt and seen. In himself, and between himself, the family and Joan. In his thoughts about what had happened between Joan and Webster. On other mornings he would not have cared to see what Hackett, the buyer and the prize fighter were doing. Now he was interested. In Hackett especially. In trying to remember exactly what Hackett had said to him that morning, with the foreman outside the hoodlum wagon waiting for him to get up and come out.

It had been something about shooting the foreman. Now he had it: "Pull that pepperbox you've got in your pants pocket." And, "He wears his gun for scenery," which carried the implication that the foreman was not a formidable man with such a weapon. Most important was the impression he had got out of Hackett's suggestion—that Hackett himself was a secret enemy of the foreman's and would not regret seeing, or having, him killed. And that Hackett lacked the courage to do the deed. Not much courage would be required, if Webster was slow in handling a gun—if he used a gun only for scenery. Dade needed only a gun for himself and an opportunity to use it, and no friend of Webster's to witness the murder. With Webster gone he could manage Joan and send the family back East.

He had not seen Mona and Gregg at breakfast and he thought they must still be in their rooms. He went back to his own room and waited there, listening. At length he heard a step in the hall and opened his door a little to peep out, just in time to see Mona entering the living room. He went slowly through the living room and saw Mona in the dining room, just taking a chair at the table. He wondered where Gregg was and thought he had probably gone out to meet Kelso. He was always with the prize fighter. But Kelso was sitting with the cattle buyer, so Gregg hadn't left the house as yet. He might still be in his room.

He lounged to the front door and looked out upon the veranda, to see only vacant chairs where the family had been. Then he saw them walking slowly eastward in some timber, close together, as if talking. Talking about him, he supposed. Laughing at him. He crossed the veranda and stood at its edge, still feeling the tension that seemed to have settled everywhere like an atmosphere. He had been shoved out of all their lives. He was an alien who did not understand their language or share in their plans. He was not wanted here, Gail had said, claiming to repeat Joan's words. Was that a lie told by Gail? No; that was the truth. Joan herself had told him the same thing, in effect. He was a pariah, despised and ignored, and he felt that way. Threatened by Webster; scorned by Joan; treated with contempt by the family. They had made it all plain enough. They had made sure he would understand. The way he now felt was the way he had sometimes felt when his pockets were empty after a night at the gambling tables. But he had not held the resentment he now held. There was more at stake here. Money, and a sudden malignant hate. That hate sent him down from the veranda into the dust of the yard. Yet as he walked toward the stable he found himself wondering what strange urge was pushing him, and why he was not resisting it—why he was not so cold and nerveless as he had always been. He was astonished to realize that everything seemed strange to him this morning, and he blamed the light, which he thought to be unusually glaring, bringing objects into bold and sharp relief. There was no softness anywhere, no retreating perspectives. The buildings loomed big and close; distances were deceptive, and there was a strange bleakness walking with him, and pallid thoughts taking no form.

He came close to the foreman's shack and saw the buyer and the prize fighter sitting there on the door sill, close together, looking at him with expressionless eyes; and Hackett, leaning against a wall of the building, smoking a pipe, sucking it slowly, one hand holding the bowl, the other hooked into the cartridge belt around his waist.

Only Hackett spoke to him; the others merely looked at him. Hackett said, "Well, it's the Duke!" But Hackett's voice had a flat sound, for there was no feeling in the greeting.

"Hello, Hackett," he said and saw the buyer and the prize fighter get up, stretch themselves and walk toward the stable, opposite the shack. That action added something to the strangeness of the atmosphere, which seemed to move with him, wherever he went, and to the tension, because their manner told him plainly enough that the feeling against him here ran through all of them. Until the last few days they had treated him civilly enough.

He rolled and lit a cigarette and saw his hands shaking, so that he spilled the tobacco.

"Nerves going?" said Hackett, unsmiling.

Dade leaned against the wall of the shack and rolled another smoke, finishing it this time and lighting it. His hands were steadier.

"Nerves are all right, Hackett," he said.

"Must have been—to bring you here," said Hackett. "To this country." He glanced sidelong at Dade, his face long, his voice low. Lathrop and Kelso were near but were slowly moving away. "Heard the news?" Hackett said. "I see you have," he added when Dade looked at him.

"That news is straight then," said Dade. "He has hooked her."

"She's been nibbling a long time," said Hackett. He drew on his pipe and sent a cloud of smoke out of a corner of his mouth into Dade's face. Dade fanned the smoke with a hand and wondered if the action signified contempt. He could tell nothing from Hackett's expression. "He's been so damned slow, though," said Hackett, thinking of Webster. "He might have had her long ago—if he had had the gumption."

"You said something about him once before," said Dade. "At your camp in Bear Flat. I was in the hoodlum wagon. Webster was standing there. Remember? Something about him not having nerve."

"Did I?" said Hackett. He watched Lathrop and Kelso go to the stable door and stand there. He heard them laugh and his own lips seemed to twitch in sympathy— a dry, drooping smile. The smile stayed on his lips as he looked at the gambler. "Why, yes," he said, "that's right. I always thought he lacked nerve—in some things. I've told him that."

"That took courage—didn't it?" said Dade.

"To tell him?" said Hackett. He had looked away, but now he looked back to study Dade's face. "I've told him worse things than that," he said.

"And he took them?"

"Like a little man," said Hackett.

"He must be afraid of you," said Dade.

Frost suddenly filled Hackett's eyes and the gambler's mouth jerked open. "What's that?" said Hackett. "What you getting at?"

"Don't lose your temper now," soothed Dade. "It was something you said at your Bear Flat camp. It made me think of that."

"So you've been thinking?" said Hackett. "When?" he asked. "Before or since?"

"Before or since when?" said Dade in a small voice.

"Before or since Joan found out it was Webster she wanted," said Hackett. "And before or since you came here? Or any time!" He took the pipe out of his mouth, knocked the ashes from it and put it into a pocket. It was a small, conical stone pipe with a long reed stem, and before putting it into the pocket he held it by its extreme end and waggled the bowl at Dade. "What are you thinking now?" he said. "You're talking about nerve but you ain't got any. If you'd had any nerve you'd have shot Webster before now—for horning in and taking Joan away from you."

"I'm going to shoot him," said Dade.

Hackett looked at the ground and at Lathrop and Kelso standing in front of the stable door; at the sky which was now a shimmering white blur; at the corral fences forming their giant rectangles, and then at his pipe which he took from the pocket in which he had placed it, holding it in his hands and turning it over and over, feeling the bowl which was hot from the previous smoking; at last filling it, lighting it and meditatively puffing at it. "What got that idea into your head?" he said.

"You," said Dade. "What you said at your Bear Flat camp while Webster was waiting for me to get out of the hoodlum wagon. You told me to shoot him. Remember?"

"Maybe I did," said Hackett. "Sometimes I've wanted to shoot him myself." He looked Dade over with critical eyes and added, "What are you going to shoot him with? That derringer you carry in your pants pocket? Or maybe you're going to cut him up with the knife you keep in that sheath under your belt."

"He took my knife and gun away from me," said Dade.

"He did! I didn't hear anything about that. How? He don't talk much."

"It was when he was taking me to the ranch house with him, the day I came. Seems he was afraid I might use them. I had to throw them into some brush."

"The damned cuss!" said Hackett. "Scared of you," he added.

"That's what I thought."

"Well, that's like him. You can never tell what he's thinking about. He'll be nice and polite to you one day, and the next day he'll pull a gun on you and blast hell out of you. If you're close to him—that is. He can't hit the stable at—oh, say a rope's length."

"What's a rope's length?"

"About forty feet."

"I'd be pretty safe at that distance, you think?"

"Yes. Sure. If you take plenty of time aiming at him. But you say you ain't got a gun." He studied the gambler's face while thinking of Webster—of how he himself had tried to imitate the foreman's smooth, lightning draw, and how he could never achieve his deadly accuracy, at any distance. The gambler was a dead man if he drew a gun on Webster—unless he did the shooting from behind. He was as good as dead right now for letting his intention become known. But this was a matter for thoughtful consideration.

Dade went toward the house and Hackett sauntered over to the stable door, joining Lathrop and Kelso there and reflectively watching Dade walk away. Hackett's pipe was still going and he puffed slowly at it. "He knows Webster has cut him out," he said and looked at the buyer. "He's got his dander up. He thinks he'll shoot Webster."

"Whew!" said Lathrop. He watched Dade for a moment. "The damned fool!" he said. "Did you tell him that? Did he ever see Webster throw a gun?"

"I'll bat his ears off!" said Kelso.

"No," said Hackett. "That wouldn't end it. He'd still have poison in him. Now, look. He has gone on for eleven years thinking his thoughts. He couldn't have thought such thoughts for that long in this country. Somebody would have busted them out of him. So he's lived longer than he should have lived. Why didn't he stay away from here? Why did he come back to mess things up again?"

"Too bad for Webster," said Lathrop. "You'll warn him when he comes in?"

"It would spoil things to have Webster kill him," said Hackett. "She'd think there would be no need for that. She might hold it against him. He'll have to be kept out of the way so she'll know he had no hand in it." He saw Dade step upon the veranda and go into the house. The family was still far up the road, near the timber, and was still walking away. Mona was coming toward the stable. Gregg had not come out of the house. "Joan and Webster were riding to hold a powwow with Spotted Elk this morning," Hackett went on. "They were to settle about the beef ante and the killing of them braves by Gumbo and his boys. Spotted Elk is old and don't want any trouble, but his braves were getting out of hand. They were yelling for dances and war paint. But yesterday a detail from Fort McDowell, under Lieutenant Dundon, herded them together and headed them for that new reservation just this side of old Fort Whipple. Webster had sent for the soldiers, not wanting any more trouble before the fall roundup. Webster knew the soldiers were coming, so he and Joan didn't ride in that direction. I rode in to make sure they wouldn't, and that makes things just right."

XXIII

Dade went into the house and stood for a while in front of the big mantel in the living room, listening, wondering where Gregg was and thinking about Mona. Thinking of how, if his plans went through, he'd knock some of the nonsense out of the boy. Thinking of the smile Mona had given him as she had passed him on her way to go to the stable where Hackett and Lathrop and Kelso were standing—a slight placid smile, yet it gave him an impression of deep and contemptuous mockery and satisfaction. They all resented his presence here.

He went into his room and searched the drawers in the bureau there. Not finding what he wanted, he went out and down the hall to the south window, where he saw that Mona had joined Hackett and the others in front of the stable. Faint laughter reached him and twisted his lips with rage. He went into Mona's room and Joan's, where sight of dresses and feminine finery there sent a nostalgic pang through him, reminding him of associations that were no longer attainable. He searched the dresser, where he might find what he wanted, and went out into the hall again, going from one room to another until he had searched all of them. There remained only Gregg's room, and when he opened the door and looked in he saw Gregg propped up in bed, his right elbow resting upon a pillow, looking straight at him out of sleep-dimmed eyes. But the boy had been listening to him as he had prowled through the other rooms, for his eyes—reminding Dade of Joan's—were accusingly keen and probing.

"Are you looking for Mother?" he said. "She's gone riding with Bob Webster."

"You've got too much gab," said Dade, his hate stirred by the boy's words. And he had not forgotten Gregg's reluctance in the handshaking incident on the day of his arrival here, and the boy's persistent avoidance of all personal contact with him afterward. And he had seen how Gregg had watched him during the following days, his thoughts deep and meditatively hostile. This was the first time he had been alone with the boy, and he stood there studying him, enjoying his helplessness. He knew his hate must be visible and he wondered why Gregg did not cringe under it.

"I heard you walking about," said Gregg. "Tiptoeing. I wondered what you were doing."

"You did, eh?" Dade said. "Suspicious, were you?"

"No," said Gregg, sitting up, smiling. This man was his father, though he did not like him very much—not at all, in fact, though he had tried to like him, and wanted to like him, if he could. "I just wondered what you wanted," he said.

"It wasn't your mother," said Dade. He moved away from the door and closer to the bed. He stood looking down at the boy, studying his face to see if he could find in it any resemblance to his own. It was all Joan—all

224

Parlette. Even to the serenity of the eyes which were steadily returning his stare. That steadiness annoyed him, irritated him. The kid ought to show some affection—diffidence at least. The rage that surged up in him was like a strong wine, warming his blood which the hostile atmosphere around here had chilled. Even his own kid was against him! He said, "How often does your mother go riding with Webster?"

"Not often," said Gregg. "Only when they have to go somewhere on business."

"Where have they gone now?" said Dade.

"Not very far," said the boy, remembering his mother's words. "Only to some places she has almost forgotten, she said."

"Sentimental, isn't she?" said Dade.

"Sir?" said Gregg, thinking he meant some slighting reference to his mother.

"Don't 'sir' me!" said Dade. "I don't want any of your damned politeness. How soon will she be back?"

"I don't know. She said I shouldn't miss going to the padre for my lessons. But she won't stay long. She never does."

"You like Webster—don't you?" said Dade.

"Sure."

"But you don't like me," said Dade. "Not as a father or as a man? Well, you don't need to, right now. But one of these days I'll teach you a thing or two. Understand that?"

"Yes." Gregg stared at him. "I ought to like you," he said. "For you are my father." He was puzzled because he felt no remorse for his lack of affection. "I am trying to like you," he said. "I don't know why I don't like you."

Dade said, "Hell! You're just as fickle as your mother!"

The boy's eyes grew hotly resentful. "Don't you talk that way about my mother!" he said.

"No?" said Dade. "Don't get fresh or I'll knock your face off! I've wanted to. You've got too much lip anyway." Once more he was puzzled because Gregg did not wince or cringe. He said, "Where is that gun you've been wearing?"

Gregg looked at an empty gun belt and holster hanging on the wall above his head. "My gun is gone," he said. "The trigger spring is broken. The blacksmith is going to put a new one in. It will take him a day or two. He's awful busy, and the steel has to be tempered just right."

"Is that the only gun you've got?"

"Yes," said Gregg. He was trying to be friendly. "You never wear a gun—do you?" he said. "Is it because you don't know how to use one?" He smiled at Dade. "It's right not to wear a gun if you don't know how to use it," he added. "A man wearing a gun won't shoot a man who doesn't wear one—unless he's a murderer."

"Look here," said Dade. "I don't want to listen to any damned lecture by a kid! I don't want a gun. But I thought, with Indians running around the country, there ought to be a lot of guns handy."

"The riders wear them," said Gregg. "Some of them

wear two. And sometimes, when the Indians are bothering, the gardeners wear them. They all carry rifles too. Mother has a six-shooter. It's swell and she hides it from me. But when she goes riding she carries it. She wore one of Grandfather's guns once. She says Grandfather never missed with it." He screwed his brows together. "Did you know my grandfather—John Parlette?" he asked.

"I know all the Parlettes I want to know," said Dade. "Where does she keep that gun?"

"She don't hide that one from me," said Gregg. "Or from anybody. It's in a holster that hangs alongside the mantel in the living room. The stock is awkward for me to handle. It's too big for my hand. But my grandfather liked it. He killed lots of Indians with it. He was a great man. Don't you think so?"

"Because he killed Indians?" said Dade. "Hell, what's killing a few Indians!" He stared hard into the boy's eyes. Just like hers, he thought, and remembered how she had looked at him when she had told him he was no longer wanted here. "What kind of a gun is it?" he said. "I've never noticed it hanging there."

"It's kind of old," Gregg explained. "But it will go plenty hard. It's a Texas pistol called the 'Peacemaker.' It was one of the first central-fire pistols. It's a single-action .45-caliber. It holds six cartridges but it's liable to go off if you don't have one empty cylinder to let the hammer down on."

Dade had seen weapons of the type described by Gregg. He remembered their owners had said they were reliable. So his search was ended, and he stood looking at the boy, the tension relieved now that he had means of defending himself, and means of killing Webster. None of them had any rights here—the family, or Webster. They were making a "play" for Joan's money, that was all. And if they got her money they would get it at his expense. Gregg wasn't important but he was a Parlette, Joan's son and Webster's friend. That the boy was striving to conquer his dislike and distrust of his father made no difference. Rather, the fact that there was dislike and distrust to overcome made it all the more certain that it was there. It was bred into him, and he could never throw it off. He was a hypocrite for trying to conquer his real feelings. A sudden cruel impulse brought a twisting droop to Dade's lips, and he walked back and forth beside the bed, looking at Gregg but thinking of Joan. In the hall yesterday, talking with her, he had wanted to strike her, to knock the independence out of her; had wanted to drive the contemptuous calmness and the smug serenity out of her eyes; had wanted to smash the lips that, once so sweet to him, had pronounced the final words of their estrangement. The way she had looked at him—bravely and steadily—was the way Gregg was looking at him now, seeing the cruel hardness in his eyes and on his twisting lips—knowing he was hated.

Dade stepped to the side of the bed and looked down at the boy who was sitting erect, looking up at him, the way Joan had looked at him yesterday—calmly, with a little wonder and no fear.

"So you don't like me?" he said. "And you are trying to be a damned hypocrite about it. All this talk about *trying* to like me! That's the bunk! She told you not to like me—didn't she?"

"You mean my mother? That she taught me not to like you? That isn't so!" said Gregg and shook his head in positive negation. "She hasn't said anything to me about you," he added. "She hasn't even mentioned you."

Dade said, "She'll mention me after today," and leaned over the bed, his face close to the boy's. It was odd how his nearness to the boy inflamed him. How his knowledge of the boy's helplessness urged him, deepened his sense of the wrong he felt had been done him by Joan, drove him to a fury of self-pity and blinding, reeling rage. "You'll mention me after today too," he said. "You'll obey me and treat me with respect, or I'll knock hell out of you!"

Hurting the kid would hurt her. She would feel the blows. It was almost as if she were sitting there, watching him, cringing. But not pleading, not begging him to withhold his hand.

"You won't hit me!" said Gregg, sitting up straighter, startled. "You wouldn't dare to hit me!"

Dade slapped the boy's face with an open hand, viciously, with the cruel intent of savage rage. With unusual clarity he saw the boy's startled eyes and rocking head; the welt prints of his fingers on the smooth skin of his cheek; the blood trickle welling from his lips. He had intended striking only once. But when, standing over Gregg, he saw how the boy braced himself with his hands to keep from toppling over, and how there came into his eyes a light of bitter scorn and contempt and taunting defiance, he struck again and again with open hand and with fist, until the boy was beaten to the pillow and huddled there with closed eyes, his cheeks and lips macerated, with blood from his wounds running down from his chin, staining his night robe and the bedclothing.

"There!" said Dade. Rage made him breathe heavily. What he had done appalled him. He stepped back, shaking. "I'll teach you to defy me, you confounded brat!" he said in self-justification. He hadn't intended to hit so hard. The boy might be dead. He moved forward fearfully and peered into Gregg's face, and was relieved when he saw that the boy was still breathing, that his eyes were still closed and were fluttering. He retreated to the closed door and stood there, fearfully watching the boy, listening, wiping his hands with a handkerchief, seeing bloodstains upon them.

He had not thought that this would happen. The tension surrounding him had done this to him. And now that tension was greater than ever, for the thing he had done just now was showing him that his emotions were unstable and that he must watch himself.

XXIV

He went into the living room and stood beside the big mantel there, examining the gun Gregg had told him about—the Peacemaker. His hands were still shaking as

230

he removed the cylinder pin of the weapon, took the cylinder out, removed the cartridges, replaced the empty cylinder, cocked the hammer and snapped it upon the empty chambers. It worked perfectly. It was a heavy gun with a walnut stock. It looked, and felt, serviceable. He reloaded it, leaving out one cartridge and letting the hammer down upon the empty chamber, and stuck the gun inside the waistband of his trousers, under his shirt, to conceal it. For a moment he stood near the mantel looking at the gun rack in which were several rifles—one of them a Winchester of fine make which he suspected belonged to Joan. He wondered if the rifles, like the revolver, were loaded and took down the Winchester, to find five cartridges in it—four in the magazine and one in the firing chamber. He worked the drop-lever action, unloading and reloading it. "Ready for use," he said. "Ready for Indians." And left the rack to go out upon the veranda where he stood for a minute looking about him. He saw the family coming back toward the house, and Mona and Kelso in one of the corrals. He could see only the heads of the two in the corral, but he caught occasional glimpses of the loops of a rope running sinuously out as the fighter aimed at a snubbing post in the corral. He had seen Gregg and the fighter at their rope tricks. He knew of their friendship and wondered what the fighter would do if he knew what had happened to Gregg. That had been an astonishing thing—the boy making no sound, refusing to acknowledge the pain of the beating he had received, his eyes steady and indomitable. And no moaning afterward. The Parlette spirit, he supposed—Joan's spirit. The spirit which had rejected him after he had injured her, in another way. He saw the buyer and Hackett perched upon the high adobe wall of one of the cattle corrals. They seemed to be looking at some steers there and talking about them. But Hackett was also watching the surrounding country for Joan and Webster to intercept the foreman so that Dade would have no opportunity to do his shooting.

Hackett looked toward the ranch house and saw Dade sitting on the edge of the veranda, and the family just reaching there. "She sure fell into a den of rattlers," he said.

"Who?" said Lathrop. "Oh yes—the family and Dade." He turned and looked at the house. "So you've been keeping an eye on him?" he said, speaking of the gambler.

"He stayed in the house for a while," said Hackett. "A long while. Then he came out and walked up and down and finally settled where he is. He gets up and walks around and then goes back and sits down again. Nervous. But he's got what he was looking for."

"What's that?" said Lathrop. He looked at Hackett.

"A gun," said Hackett. He grinned at the buyer. "How do I know he's got a gun?" he said. "That's what you are bug eyed about? He's got it inside the waistband of his pants. He's been fanning it every once in a while to make sure it's there." He looked into the north country and toward the padre's hacienda. "Gregg's late for his lessons," he added. "He couldn't have gone to the

232

padre's place without me seeing him. That brush along the road might hide him until he got to the stable, but he couldn't get past there without showing himself. It's funny that Kelso ain't been to the house to get him up. He's usually hanging around there."

"Webster and Joan are staying long," said the buyer. "Well, I don't blame them. That's a pretty country over there—where they went. Best thing is—they're alone. With each other. They'll enjoy that."

Hackett swung around and got ready to drop from the wall. "They're coming now," he said. "Over there—in that swale. The sage there is knee-high and turning purple." He pointed and the buyer looked.

"They are taking their time," said the buyer. "They don't know what's ahead of them."

"You meaning marriage or Dade?" said Hackett and dropped to the ground.

They walked along the corral fence, Hackett keeping Dade and Webster and Joan in sight, and reached the rear of the stable where both men stopped and watched the approach of the couple in whom their chief interest lay. The lovers were riding leisurely, but their slow pace finally brought them to the front of the big stable where Hackett and the buyer met them. Hackett caught Webster's eye and drooped the lid of one of his own as he spoke to Joan. He said, "Lieutenant Dundon and a troop of cavalry rode into Bear Flat yesterday. The lieutenant sent his respects to you and told me to assure you that Spotted Elk and his braves will not bother you again. They're going to that new reservation."

"Wonderful!" she said. "Tom, you are always so reliable and dependable!" she laughed. "And I think you remembered the lieutenant's words remarkably well."

"So you think it sounded like him, eh?" said Hackett. He grinned. "But I had a tough time remembering. I'm getting slow, Miss Joan." He was thinking of how he should have found an excuse to shoot Dade while at Bear Flat. Had he shot him then, he would not be facing the task of shooting him now, with all the family around to be horrified and critical. Her word, that time, had stopped him. "Slow now," he said, "and not polite, or I wouldn't be asking you to ride on to the house while I tell Bob Webster something Lieutenant Dundon told me to tell him. Miguel will go up and bring your horse back." He looked again at the house and saw Dade walking back and forth in front of it.

Joan thanked him and rode on, throwing a kiss to Webster, who scowled at Hackett as he slid out of the saddle. "It had better be important," said Webster, facing Hackett at the stable door. Lathrop walked away toward the foreman's shack.

While Hackett and Webster talked Lathrop dropped to the doorsill and sat there watching Joan as she dismounted at the veranda, where the family had gathered, having seen her ride in with Webster. Dade was now sitting at the far edge of the veranda, his back to a big adobe column. He was watching Webster and Hackett and would have given much to have known what they were talking about. He wanted to catch Webster off guard—in his shack if possible. It wouldn't be too bad, either, if he had to kill the buyer—and he would do just that if he could catch them together in the shack. He would wait until after dark, though, unless between now and then an opportunity should come.

He saw Webster and Hackett walk to the mess house where Lathrop joined them. They were inside a long time, and when they emerged Lathrop went again to the foreman's shack while Webster and Hackett crossed to the stable. They were far in the rear of the building when Dade saw the padre riding toward the house. He was near the house when Webster and Hackett saw him, with only his back visible to them, and his horse was in a slow jog. Kelso and Mona had finished the rope throwing and were near the house. The fighter waved a hand to the padre, who waved back. Webster and Hackett moved on through the stable and out of the front door to the road, where Hackett stopped and stared at the veranda which the padre was just reaching.

"He's aiming to find out why Gregg didn't come to him for his lessons," Hackett said. "He never lets the kid miss them."

Lathrop came to the door of the foreman's shack and seated himself on the sill again. From inside the shack he had watched the padre ride past while Webster and Hackett were in the rear of the stable, and he had seen something he thought he had better not mention—the padre's worried eyes and his nervous jerking while riding. He had been talking too—talking to himself, and Lathrop had caught a few words: "I hope he isn't sick." But Lathrop said nothing as Webster and Hackett approached and stood near, continuing their talk.

"So he feels *that* poisonous?" said Webster.

"I don't know how much of his talk was wind," said Hackett. "But I had to tell you. Not knowing what is in his mind, you might turn your back to him." He watched Webster's face and saw his lips tighten and a chill come into his eyes. "You remember I was wanting to blow him apart at Bear Flat," he said. "So you can see that when you postpone a thing like that—knowing it's got to be done because sooner or later his thoughts will drive him to do something foolish—you're just piling up trouble for other folks. Awhile ago, when he was airing his notions, I would have talked plain to him. But he had no gun on him. He's got one now in the waistband of his pants."

Here was something of which the buyer had knowledge. He added a word to Hackett's. "It ain't your funeral—unless you want to become one of the mourners," he said to Webster. "Right now you're grade A with her. Shooting him now would spoil things for you."

"She'd do some serious thinking," argued Hackett softly. "Thoughts would bother her. If you'd kill him she'd see him every time she looked at you. And that would take something out of what you'd have a right to expect from her." He drew out his pipe and filled it, winked at the buyer while lighting it and jerked his head slightly toward the door of the shack. "There'll be time enough to decide about it," he said. "It will take him days and days, maybe, to screw his courage up to the point where he'll even look at you."

"Thinking it over will show him how foolish he is," said the buyer. "Then he'll ride back to Tucson, feeling that running a faro table is safer. Anyhow, you can't go right up there and give him his chance, with Joan and the family there looking at you." He got up from the doorsill, his sly eyes rolling, a smile breaking the set expression of his lips. He said, "Did I tell you that I've decided to give you the price you've been holding out for? Thirty. This time it all goes to the boss. It's bad business, but I suppose I've got to let you have your way. Come on in and we'll do some figuring."

Dade was now thinking he had made a mistake in hitting Gregg. The incident had added something to the bleakness of this day, and had stirred him to a furtive watchfulness which caused him to study the faces around him, to attempt to discover if they knew what had happened to the boy. It had brought to him a dread of meeting Kelso, of being near the fighter when the story of the incident became known, as it would be, sooner or later. He did not care so much about the rest of them, and if Webster should take Gregg's end of the affair, the differences between the foreman and himself would be settled quickly.

Back from a nervous walk around the house, he slid into a sitting position on the edge of the veranda, his back to the big adobe corner column, and listened to the family and watched what was going on around him. He saw Webster and Joan ride in and stop in front of the stable; saw Joan come on toward the house while Webster got out of the saddle and turned his horse over to old Miguel, and then stood there in front of the stable door with Hackett and Lathrop. Mona and Kelso were coming toward the house from the corral, but he pretended not to see Joan as she rode up and dismounted, blushing a little, to be greeted with, "So you didn't ride to Bear Flat after all?" from Kathleen and, "Didn't you know Tom Hackett was coming in?" from Gail.

Joan stood on the edge of the great porch after getting out of the saddle and smiled at her sisters, and at Paul, who silently watched her, thinking that she grew more beautiful each day. The flush on her face, he thought, was from riding in the sun. But her hair, disordered by the wind, was glorious, and he had never seen her eyes so expressive. They were dancing with mysterious soft lights. He had not seen her like this.

"Yes," she said to Gail, "I knew Tom was riding in. No," she said, answering Kathleen, "we didn't ride to Bear Flat. And we knew we were riding in the wrong direction. Were you worrying about us?"

Kathleen and Gail did not reply and Joan went into the house. The veranda was silent for a long time, and Dade watched Hackett and Webster go into the stable, and Lathrop into the foreman's shanty. The fighter and Mona were now very close to the house. Then the padre appeared on the road between the stable and the house while Hackett and Webster were behind the stable. Dade had not thought of Gregg going for his lessons, and he watched the padre intently, suspecting that the cleric had come to inquire about the absence of his pupil.

Dade looked across the veranda at the sisters. They had not improved their relations with the padre and the gambler was somehow glad they hadn't, for when he saw worry in the padre's eyes as he drew his horse up at the veranda and sat there in the saddle interrogating all of them with one inclusive glance, it was apparent that Gregg was on his mind and that presently what had happened to the boy would be known.

The padre said quietly, "Do any of you know where I might find Gregg? He hasn't been to my house for his lessons."

Kathleen said, "Why, I haven't seen the boy. Not at breakfast or since. I don't see why Joan doesn't take better care of him. If he belonged to me I certainly wouldn't let him run around with that prize fighter."

Mona and Kelso were now standing at the edge of the veranda. Mona said, "The Lord knows why he didn't let you have a boy—or anything," and smiled at Kelso, who grinned appreciatively. "You say Gregg hasn't been to you for his lessons?" added Mona. She frowned. "I haven't seen him either," she said. "That's strange. He's always around, somewhere." She stepped to the veranda, but the padre had already dismounted and was crossing to the door where he stopped and looked back, smiling.

"There's nothing to be worried about, I am sure," he said. "He has probably overslept. He will be out here presently." He found a chair and sat in it. His eyes roved from the door to Mona, who was watching the sisters and Paul; and to Kelso, standing at the veranda edge, brushing dust from his short-sleeved shirt. He leaned back in the chair and saw Hackett and Webster and the buyer standing near the foreman's shack. They were facing the house and he thought they were watching something of interest to them. He was looking at Dade when he heard a sound from the living room and Gregg's voice calling, "Mother! Mother!" There was some sort of an appeal there, of special urgency, and though the padre started out of his chair at the call, he saw the gambler's face whiten as he stared through the door into the living room. The padre, farthest from the door, was last of them all to see Gregg as he reached the door and stood there looking at them.

"Is Mother here?" he said. "I thought I heard her talking."

His face, puffed and bruised, showed the angry welts raised by Dade's fingers. He was trying to smile, but his lips were awry and grotesque from the macerating blows he had received, and smeared with the blood that had dried upon them. The padre was moving toward him as he said, his voice husky with pity, "Gregg! Oh, my son!" and dropped to his knees beside the boy and held him tight and gently patted his shoulders. Gregg was silent, returning the padre's caresses, but his eyes were as steady and brave as they had been while Dade had been beating him. The sisters gasped and cried out and sat rigid, their faces set with horror and shock; Paul half rose from his chair and cursed and looked at Dade; Mona screamed "My God!" as she stared at Gregg and tried to reach him, the padre holding her off, trying to wave them all to silence. Kelso, at the veranda edge, stood with lips tight shut, looking at Dade. Old Miguel, arriving to take Joan's horse back to the stable, had started to lead the animal away but got only as far as the east corner of the house where he, too, stopped to stare and to mutter.

They were all standing now and peering at Gregg as the padre held him. They all saw Joan darting through the living room to the door. She had changed from her riding clothes to a house dress which was open at the throat as if she had been disturbed before having an opportunity to button it. Dressing, she had heard the padre's loud cry, but she had not thought it would be Gregg he had been talking to, knowing that at this moment the boy should be at the padre's house. Her hair, half combed, was in jumbled waves and coils, shapeless and formless, and was sagging in loops and folds halfway to her shoulders, with loose strands negligently dangling, framing her white face and anxious eyes as she appeared in the doorway. She caught her breath as she stood there, her eyes bright and wild with dismay and apprehension, and cried out, "Gregg! Oh, Gregg! My dear!" and folded him in her arms as he turned to her.

She stood there with the boy and hugged him; and held him away from her a little as she ran exploring fingers over the bruises and welts on his face; and shuddered and cried softly, and repeated, "Oh, Gregg, Gregg, my dear," in a hushed voice; and hugged him again and kissed his lips and cheeks, and turned her back to all of them so that they could not see. The sisters, shocked to silence, were hovering near, white of face; Mona was crying, forgetting for once to be sarcastic to the family; the padre's face was stern and cold, and he was looking at Webster and Hackett and the buyer, who had been standing in front of the foreman's shack but were now walking at an accelerated pace toward the house, having seen the commotion on the veranda. Kelso, slowly edging his way toward Dade, who was now standing near the big adobe column, was gritting his teeth. They all heard Joan's voice as she said to Gregg, "What was it, dear? What happened to you? Please tell Mother. No one will hurt you again."

Gregg drew an arm free and pointed at Dade, but none of those on the veranda, or Kelso, standing beside it, showed any surprise. And Dade, with the boy's accusing finger pointing him out, seemed to shrink a little. "He—Father—Mr. Dade, hit me," said Gregg. "I was in bed. I was just getting ready to go to the padre for my lessons. I heard Mr. Dade going through the other rooms. He came into my room and talked to me. He was looking for a gun. Then he hit me—a lot of times."

Joan shook her head and shuddered and held Gregg tighter. "Oh!" she said in a smothered voice. She looked at Dade, whose face whitened. He was beginning to understand that the blows he had given the boy were now hurting her, and that he had repaid her for rejecting him, which had been his intention. But there was something here that he had not foreseen, and which, perhaps, he could not understand—the hold of the boy on the affections of all of them. He saw Mona had stopped crying and was watching him with hate implacable. The sisters were looking at him, too, their chins held high, contempt in their eyes. Kelso was staring at him, a sinister smirk on his lips, his gaze steady, unblinking. Hackett and Webster were here, too, now. Webster had stepped to Joan's side, had whispered something to her and to Gregg, and had then moved to the office door where he leaned against one of the jambs, folded his arms and looked at Dade, and listened to Joan as she talked to Gregg.

Yes, there was something here, and Dade began to hear it—an unvoiced threat, a ringing around him of a menacing circle, tightening, growing narrower. A chill began to creep over him, and the sun beating down upon him gave him no warmth. The padre walked slowly to the edge of the veranda and stood there for a time looking at Joan and Gregg, who were now whispering to each other; at Webster leaning against the doorjamb, his arms folded, his chin on his chest; and at Hackett and Kelso waiting there, saying nothing.

Joan saw them too—all of them. How Webster's eyes, frosty, squinting, shifted from Gregg to Dade and back to the boy with definite comprehension and cold purpose; and how Hackett stood facing Dade, his lips in a set grin of rage and contempt. Their feelings and emotions she could understand, but her own were deeper and more involved. In them, while she cried softly over Gregg, she traced the pattern of her eleven-year experience, beginning with Dade and ending with the bruised and beaten face of her boy—and his.

Watching her from the door of the foreman's office, where he waited—waited as all of them waited—for a word from her, Webster understood and held up a hand to stop all movement. Hackett slid to a sitting posture on the edge of the veranda and stared hard at her, amazed to see how greatly she resembled her father, and how quiet she was, like him, in moments of deep feeling. The padre, who knew her as well as he had known her parents, looked at Dade and slowly wagged his head from side to side. He knew all the riders of the Parlette range, too, and was certain that, though Dade's treatment of Joan might be forgiven by them, their punishment for the beating he had given Gregg would be swift and merciless. These men here, Webster and Hackett, would not kill Dade in Joan's presence so they listened and watched and nursed their hate of the man, and saw how, gradually, the gambler was beginning to understand what was in their minds.

The word they were waiting for was coming. Joan stood erect and looked at Dade. What little color still remained in her cheeks was draining away. A small, pale, twisting smile twitched at her lips as she saw Dade cringe, and her hands, which had been hanging at her sides, began to come up—the left finally reaching her throat which was throbbing; the right to brush her cascaded hair back from her forehead. The fury in her eyes was so deep and cold that it made Hackett's breath catch in his throat and choke him. Her lips were tight with bitterness. The fighter, who knew frenzy when he saw it, whispered, "Holy gee!"

Her look, though, was upon Dade only, and he began to retreat from her. Then he stopped and leaned toward her, and it seemed as if he was waiting for her to speak. He waited there as she gently pushed Gregg away from her into Mona's arms. When she suddenly turned and went through the door into the living room he swayed uncertainly and ran back to the adobe column where he stood, his knees shaking. He was hoping this would be the end of it—that her frenzy would dissolve in tears, when he heard the padre, near him, saying, "May God have mercy on you!" and knew it wasn't the end. His throat closed in terror when Joan suddenly appeared in the doorway just back of the threshold, throwing a rifle up to bear upon him; and with the intense vision which is sometimes given men in extreme danger he saw the stock of the weapon lying against her bare throat and her cold eyes glaring at him over the sights. He yelled as he dodged behind the corner column. As the rifle crashed a chunk of adobe clay as big as his fist burst from a corner of the column, shoulder high, on him.

He started to run, away from the veranda and down the road toward the stable, looking back over his shoulder to see Webster holding Joan tight, gun and arms, preventing her from shooting again. He whined with fright when he saw Kelso coming after him and tried to jerk the Peacemaker out—stopping that when Kelso gained on him. Then he saw Hackett following the fighter, and old Miguel riding Joan's horse.

• • •

Webster got Joan into the living room, after she had hugged Gregg and cried over him again, and the padre had stood in front of her to tell her he was glad her bullet hadn't struck Dade, and Mona had solemnly kissed her, and the family, silent and chastened, tried to look distressed and sympathetic. Joan was steady now, and clear eyed and outwardly calm, though as she stood in the rear of the living room, holding tightly to Webster, she was bracing herself for what she knew would come. She would not turn her head away from the veranda, for through the doorway she could see Gregg and Mona and the padre standing close together, facing the way Dade had gone, watching. The white sunlight beyond the shade of the veranda was ironically bright. For, permeating it, and stealing through the veranda's shade and into the living room, was the feeling of tension that had been stealing through the house all day. Only now it was stronger and more ominous, sending its forbidding message of dire things impending. They all felt it. Webster's face was grim and expectant, though he smiled at Joan. She studied his eyes and sighed. He was what she wanted—her man. Yet she thought of the other with pity at last. She was glad Webster had spoiled her aim, and her wan smile lingered upon him. And when the sounds came—one crashing, reverberating report followed instantly by two others— she began to cry. She saw Mona cover her face with her hands. Gregg was standing rigid, staring down the road. The padre was making the sign of the cross.

XXV

Hackett came into the foreman's office and dropped into a chair. He tossed his hat to the desk top, leaned back, stretched his legs and looked at Kelso and Lathrop, who entered the office with him. There had been no tension in the air Hackett had breathed. There had been no hesitation and no regret.

He found the cigar box which was always on Webster's desk and removed from it a small can of oil, a cleaner and a square of white cloth. He drew his gun from its holster on his leg, unloaded it, tossed two empty cartridges out through the door, where they rang and clattered on the stone floor of the veranda, to fall, finally, to the ground; then cleaned the cylinders and the barrel thoroughly, reloaded the weapon and let it rest on his knees as he looked at the oil painting of John Parlette on the wall facing him. He said reflectively, "You might think he was thanking me."

"What's that?" said Lathrop.

"You wouldn't know," said Hackett. "It was something between me and him there." He pointed at the painting. "He was a hellion for straight dealing."

There had been no one on the veranda when they had entered the foreman's office. They thought there was nobody in the house, for an hour had elapsed since the shooting. And when they heard voices in the living room they sat up straight and stared at one another. Lathrop nodded his head toward the outside door, indicating that perhaps they should leave, but Hackett shook his head and looked at the door of the living room which was wide open. The outside glare had blinded them momentarily, but now they could see Joan standing near the door, looking at them, and the family sitting up straight on the davenport. Webster was standing in front of the mantel; Mona was sitting in a chair near him facing the family, and the padre was standing at an end of the mantel. Joan had taken Gregg to his room where she and Mona had patched up his wounds and put him to bed.

Joan said, "Are you hurt, Tom?" and looked at Hackett. She nodded to the buyer and Kelso, who smiled at her.

Hackett ran a long forefinger through a hole in his shirt sleeve under the left arm. "He wasn't as greenhorn with a gun as he let on to be," he said. He looked at the buyer and Kelso for corroboration. "Once he got it loose from the waistband of his pants," he said. Joan was one of the people to whom he always talked straight—as he had talked to her father.

"Good gracious, Joan," said Kathleen, "you act as if there was a killing here every day! I should think you would be horrified!"

"I am," said Joan and turned to look at her sister. "And there is a limit to what one can stand. Do you know what I mean?"

"I really do not," said Kathleen.

"Her mind is a blank," said Mona.

"Must this person be present to hear what you have to

248

say to us?" said Gail. "I thought this was to be a family affair. At least that is what I gathered when you sent for us to meet you in this room."

"It *has* been a family affair," said Joan. "But this is to be the end of all such affairs here." She turned and looked at Hackett, who was shoving his gun down his leg, and at the buyer and Kelso. "Come in, please," she said. "There is something I wish to say to my sisters and my brother, and I think you ought to hear it. This is a farewell party," she added as Hackett edged into the room and the buyer and Kelso reached the door. "The family is going back East, in the station wagon, at dawn tomorrow morning, with Tom Hackett and Miguel to do the driving. I'm sure you will all miss them." Her eyes turned hard, and she was as pale as she had been on the veranda when shooting at Dade. "Tom," she said, looking at Hackett, "I have been hearing there is a story going around to the men. It's about Webster. Tell me about it, and talk straight, as you always do."

Hackett looked at Webster, at Joan and at the floor. He said, "The story is that Bob Webster has been stealing your money."

"How stealing it?" said Joan.

"By him taking five to ten dollars on every head of beef cattle bought by Lathrop," said Hackett. "By Lathrop's outfit making out two checks for each sale. One check to you and the other to Bob. It's a damn lie, Joan!" His voice shook with rage.

"Who told you about it, Tom?" said Joan.

"I heard some of the men whispering," he said. "They

had all heard the story. I finally cornered Gumbo. He said your sisters had gone through the books—through yours and Webster's. The evidence was there, they told Gumbo—sure fire." He looked at Webster. "Tell them the truth, Bob, and end it!" he said.

"That's the truth," said Webster. "Ask Lathrop."

"That's right," said the buyer and stepped in front of Hackett, who glared at Webster and himself. The sisters smiled disagreeably, and Paul smiled blandly at all of them.

"I knew Webster was guilty," said Kathleen.

"That he's been playing you for a sucker right along," said Gail.

"We were covering your hand," said Paul.

"With a four flush," said Mona. "The family bluff."

"I don't see how you could have been so blind, Joan," said Kathleen. "It must have been perfectly obvious that all Webster wanted was your money! This is the second time you have been made a fool of by unscrupulous men!"

"It's been a lot of fun for her," said Mona. "Look at what you've missed by being tough."

"You need us around here to look after you," said Gail.

"Yes," said Mona, "Joan's only a backwoods gal."

"You're out of place here, Joan," said Kathleen. "The men here are, I must say, hardly suitable for you. You seem to make unfortunate mistakes in men. First Dade, a gambler, and now this man, a thief. Come East with us, dear, and leave these people."

"But take your kale along, Joan," said Mona.

"What we have done here was for the best," said Gail. "Going through the books was a sort of hunch, you might say. And of course we couldn't understand why Mr. Lathrop should pay Bob Webster anything. And the books show he *has* paid him. Big sums too," she added. She smiled vindictively at the foreman. "Perhaps Mr. Webster has some explanation?" she said, convinced that he hadn't.

Mona looked at Webster, who was watching the family. She caught a certain gleam in the foreman's eyes and shifted her weight to the edge of her chair. "This is scrumptious!" she said. "Let the welkin ring!"

"So it is true," said Joan. She was calm and cold as she looked at the family. "You *did* start the story and you *did* go through the books. You could have only one reason, of course, and that was to discredit Bob Webster—to poison me against him so that I would discharge him. You knew I loved him, even though I didn't know it myself, and you wanted to break that up too. Isn't that right?" She gave them a pale little smile.

"Of course," said Kathleen. "We saw how things were going—that Dade would blackmail you because there hadn't been any marriage, and that Webster was stealing from you. Your *family* will not cheat or blackmail you, Joan."

"Not much," said Mona, looking at Joan. "They'd leave you a bathing suit to wear on one of the Eastern beaches—if you were lucky."

"It would have been easy to get rid of Frank Dade if

you hadn't interfered," said Joan. "And I think he would not have beaten Gregg the way he did if you hadn't put him up to it. Don't think I haven't seen how you have treated Gregg, and how you tried to make Dade hate him, right from the first day, when Paul told Dade that he would have to take Gregg in hand. You really killed Dade."

Hackett jerked erect and glared at Gail. "You was after Bob Webster too!" he said. "You stirred Dade up by making him jealous. Telling him how you'd seen Joan and Webster making love in Webster's office last night. All of you hinting that Webster should be killed, and Dade falling for it. Dade told me about it before he died. If your paw was here he'd whale the stuffing out of you!"

"There wouldn't be anything left," said Mona.

Joan's face whitened. "Oh!" she gasped, looking at Webster. "Did you know that?" She went over to him and put an arm around him.

"Tom's talking out of turn," said Webster.

"Everybody knows what I'm talking about, but nobody knows what you're thinking about," said Hackett. "You don't say anything. You just stand there like a goose looking in a bottle, looking and listening. You've got some explanation about the money you've been taking from the boss—if you *have* been taking any—but you won't open your trap."

"There is nothing to say—is there?" said Kathleen.

"It isn't always wise to talk too much," said the padre, looking at the family. "A fool is filled with words, and a suspicious person creates in others the deeds of his own imagination. There is nothing here but Bob Webster's forethought and caution. Some years ago Bob and Mr. Lathrop came to me. They explained a plan Webster had thought of. Webster was afraid that one day Frank Dade would return, and that he might squander or gamble away Joan's money and the ranch, leaving her penniless. To provide against such a misfortune Webster proposed that Lathrop should buy stock from Joan under the market price, and that the difference between the market price and the price paid to Joan should be paid to Webster, and held by me, in Joan's name, in trust. That has been done. Today every cent of the money paid to Webster by Lathrop is credited to Joan's account but held separately, in her bank in Denver, ready to be transferred to her by my signature whenever she wants it. The amount is about one hundred and fifty thousand dollars."

The padre stood motionless for a moment, looking at all of them calmly. At the sisters, whose faces had grown long and blank and suddenly old; at Paul, who was staring at the floor, his shoulders sagging; at Mona, who was smiling happily; at Hackett, who was shaking a menacing fist at Webster, and at Joan, who saw how the family had been crushed by this disclosure.

The station wagon was standing in front of the veranda, with Hackett in the driver's seat, the whip in its socket and old Miguel standing at the heads of the lead horses. Hackett's horse, unsaddled, was hitched to the tail gate by a rope hackamore. Hackett's saddle and bridle were in the wagon, up near the front. Gail and Kathleen and Paul were in the rear seats, and they kept their heads turned from the veranda where Joan and Webster and Mona and Kelso stood. Hackett would drive to Bear Flat where he would turn the reins over to Miguel, who would drive the remainder of the distance to Maricopa, convoyed by a dozen Parlette riders picked up in Bear Flat. The riders would roister in town until train time or after.

The padre stood beside the wagon and looked at the family's lengthened faces. "These partings are always hard," he said. "Even when affection has been given and received. No parting can be joyous, for something is taken away and something is left. And there is always something to be regretted."

"Yes," said Kathleen. Gail nodded silently. Paul said, "You're damned right! We were fools—thinking only of money. We forgot she was our sister. Selfishness—that's what it was."

"Not so much that perhaps," said the padre. "More a habit of thought. A way of looking at things. A way of ignoring certain human values. A way of looking down instead of looking up." He stepped back, for the horses were impatient and Hackett was looking back over his shoulder. Old Miguel was in. The padre gave Hackett the signal to go and whispered to Gail, who was closest to him, "This time, if you look down, you will find what you wanted. Gold. In the bed of the wagon. Under Hackett's saddle. At the last Joan relented. She forgives you. May you see the stars—someday—too."

The padre watched the wagon whirl away, straight into the sunlight. Then he turned and walked past the veranda toward the stable where he had left his horse, waving to Joan and Webster, who stood there, watching. Kelso and Mona had gone to Gregg's room and were now sitting on the edge of his bed talking to him.

Joan and Webster stood close together, watching the station wagon as it rolled ahead of a ballooning dust cloud about a quarter of a mile away. Suddenly the wagon stopped and the dust cloud collapsed upon and around it. Then the wind swept the dust away and the wagon and its occupants were revealed. Clearly Webster could see Hackett and Miguel in the driver's seat, and the family behind them, bending over, lifting something. Their voices floated back. They were laughing.

"They're lifting Hackett's saddle," said Webster.

"Something under the saddle," said Joan.

"Seems to tickle them," said Webster. He held her tight and looked at her. What the family had found was not important to him. The padre had told him about the gold in the wagon. More important was this—their love, and their future, together. The vast clean land, the whispering silences, the grass and the trees, and beyond and above the trees, the stars.

Center Point Publishing
600 Brooks Road ● PO Box 1
Thorndike ME 04986-0001 USA

(207) 568-3717

US & Canada:
1 800 929-9108